To Evr...
Perfect for the ...
time traveller!

SEND
SIMON
SAVAGE

Great to meet you
in sunny Australia.

All the best

Stephen Measday

SEND
SIMON
SAVAGE

Stephen Measday

Stephen Measday
2010

LITTLE 🐇 HARE
www.littleharebooks.com

Little Hare Books
an imprint of
Hardie Grant Egmont
85 High Street
Prahran, Victoria 3181, Australia

www.littleharebooks.com

Text by Stephen Measday 2010
Text copyright © Pacific Century Media Corporation 2010

First published 2010

National Library of Australia
Cataloguing-in-Publication entry

Measday, Stephen.

Send Simon Savage / Stephen Measday.

978 1 921541 33 9 (pbk.)

For primary school age.

Time travel—Juvenile fiction.

A823.3

Cover design by Xou Creative (www.xou.com.au)
Set in 11/15 pt Candida by Clinton Ellicott
Printed by Griffin Press
Printed in Adelaide, Australia, March 2010

5 4 3 2 1

This product conforms to CPSIA 2008

To
my sister and brother,
Pam Walker and Phillip Measday.
And the stories we have lived and told.
SM

1

The near future, Australia

Simon spent a great Saturday body boarding with a few mates in rolling surf at the southern end of Bondi Beach. Late in the afternoon, he headed home.

The oily smell of fish and chips hung in the air as Simon walked along the strip past the crowded cafes. He darted across the road, weaving between slow moving cars, his mind fixed on the family's usual Saturday night pig-out on fizz, pizza and cheesecake. Dodging another car, Simon jumped onto the footpath, turned up a side street, and nearly collided with old Mrs Price.

'Simon, I've never seen so much fuss!' she shouted after him. 'What's happening at your place?'

Simon blinked. 'Happening? I don't know!'

Two police cars were parked outside his house, their blue lights flashing. A group of people stood on the front porch.

He broke into a run. As he drew level with the

house, his eleven-year-old sister, Lily, burst through the gate.

'It's Dad! He's gone!' she said.

'I know. He went to work,' Simon replied.

Dad had been gone that morning when Simon got up. The night before he had promised to go surfing with Simon, but working at the weekends wasn't unusual for him. Neither was leaving for work before dawn. It happened all the time.

'No . . . really gone,' she repeated.

'What do you mean? Where?'

'They won't tell me!'

'Okay, okay. Where's Mum?'

'She's inside talking with the police. They won't let me see her!'

Simon grabbed his sister's hand, pushed through a huddle of nosy neighbours and leapt up the front steps of the house. A policeman stepped forward. 'Where are you going?'

Simon kept moving through the front door. 'Inside. We live here!'

The man stepped back and Simon dragged Lily down the hallway.

'Mum, Mum!'

He heard voices in the living room and found her talking with a policewoman.

'But you haven't found his body,' Simon's mother said. 'There's always the chance that . . .'

'Mrs Savage, we sent out a police launch,' the

policewoman replied, 'but there was a choppy sea and a strong rip off that beach. Your husband may have been washed out to sea. I'm very sorry.'

'Mum!' Simon dropped onto the couch next to his mother. 'What's going on?'

Glenda Savage gripped his hand. 'It's your father. He's . . . he's disappeared.'

It took the policewoman only a minute to tell Simon what he didn't want to know—that his father's clothes had been found on a deserted beach, about a hundred and twenty kilometres down the coast. And his car, with the keys in the ignition, was in a parking area nearby.

'The local police found a trail of footsteps in the sand, from the car right down to the water,' the policewoman said. 'We believe he swam out to sea.'

'But Dad wouldn't just swim out into a rip!' Simon said. 'That would be stupid! That would be . . . unless . . .'

'I'm sorry,' the policewoman said again.

Lily rushed to her mother's side and hugged her.

'Excuse me, are you Mrs Savage?' a deep voice said.

Simon looked up as two men in dark suits entered the room and removed their Ray-Bans. All eyes turned to them. The taller of the two was a fit, tanned and dark-haired man in his forties. He flashed an official-looking badge and photo ID.

'The name's Cutler, and this is my colleague, Anderson,' the man said, with a hint of an English accent. Then he repeated the question. 'Are you Mrs Savage?'

Glenda nodded.

The policewoman stood up. 'Excuse me,' she said. 'Who are you, exactly?'

Cutler held up his badge again. 'This is a Federal Government matter. Outside of your jurisdiction. We have a job to do, and quickly.'

The policewoman examined the distinctive metal badge and its embossed coat-of-arms. She nodded at Glenda and Simon. 'He has the authority.'

'Thank you,' Cutler replied. 'Mrs Savage, does your husband have a home office?'

'Yes.' Glenda looked towards the staircase at the far end of the room. 'His study's upstairs.'

'My apologies, but we'll have to conduct a search. This is a matter of national security.' He nodded to the other man. 'Anderson, would you take a look?'

'On my way.' Anderson moved briskly across the room and up the stairs.

Glenda took a handkerchief from her pocket and wiped the tears from her eyes. Then she looked back at Cutler with more composure. 'What are you looking for?'

'We're here to find out if your husband . . . if Dr Savage left any research papers or a personal computer here in the house,' Cutler said.

'What's that got to do with his disappearance?' Glenda asked in alarm.

Simon jumped to his feet. 'Look, Mum's really upset. Dad keeps most of his stuff at his office in the city. Or out at the research laboratory.'

'We'll be certain to look there, too,' Cutler said.

'For what?' Simon asked.

Cutler ignored him.

Then Simon noticed the man take something from his jacket pocket. It was black, the shape and size of a thick pen, and had a clear glass bubble at one end.

'You'll have to excuse me, but I need to scan everyone in the room,' Cutler explained. 'It will only take a few seconds.'

He held out the device and a thin blue beam scanned over Simon, Lily and Glenda's heads and shoulders.

'What is that thing?' Simon asked.

'A forensic testing device,' Cutler replied calmly, putting it back in his pocket.

Anderson came back down the stairs. He shook his head.

'That was quick,' Cutler remarked.

'Nothing up there of interest to us, sir,' Anderson replied.

'Well, thank you for seeing us, Mrs Savage,' Cutler said. 'We're very sorry for your loss.'

'We don't know he's lost!' Simon said. 'He might not be, you know.'

Cutler nodded. Then the two men turned and left the room as quickly as they had arrived.

'Who were those guys?' Lily asked.

Simon went to the window and watched the men get into a black car. It drove to the end of the street, nosed its way back into the traffic on the main road, and was gone.

That night, Simon couldn't sleep. Every now and then he heard some movement in his mother's bedroom, heard her blowing her nose into another tissue. But it was his own restless thoughts that kept him awake. He tried to remember every word, every movement his father had made over the last few days. He tried to find a clue as to why he had disappeared in such a strange way. And he wondered what the sudden visit from Cutler and his offsider had meant. He got out of bed and crept quietly into his dad's study.

'Simon, what're you doing?'

Lily stood in the doorway, looking pale and frail in her pyjamas.

'Just looking,' he replied.

'What for?'

'I'm checking things out,' Simon said. 'Like, why is it so tidy in here? Look, his books are all neat in the bookcases. The desk is all clear. Dad is never this tidy.'

'It smells like Dad,' Lily said. She shuffled closer to Simon.

Then, for the first time in ages, she wrapped her arms around him and held on tight. They stood like that for a long time as they stared at their father's favourite possessions.

Dr Savage's study was filled with thousands of books on science, botany, history and poetry. Many of the volumes were old and leather-bound. On the walls were framed pictures of weird flowers, like the Giant Rafflesia, which was three metres across and gave out a stink like rotten meat. A year ago, they had all gone to see one at the Botanic Gardens. And, along a dozen floor-to-ceiling shelves on the opposite wall, there were multicoloured jars of seeds and seed pods from hundreds of rare and not-so-rare plants. Collecting seeds was their dad's obsession. 'You've got to have a hobby,' he had often said.

Simon looked at the row of family photos on the mantelpiece, which sat above the fireplace that his dad had so carefully stripped and restored to its original, unpainted woodwork. His eyes lingered on the one photo that showed his father in his surfing gear. Hale Savage was a well-built man, with a full black beard, bright blue eyes and a receding hairline above a high, intelligent-looking forehead.

'He spends a lot of time in here,' Simon said at last.

'Always flat out, working on something,' Lily replied.

'Yeah, one of his big projects.'

Lily nodded.

In the last year Dad had often been tired, Simon remembered. And even a bit spaced out. Always going to his study and shutting the door. Wanting peace and quiet. But for what? Simon knew next to nothing about his father's real work. He knew it involved the atomic structure of elements and chemical compounds, and that it was new, and groundbreaking. So cutting edge, he had once joked that he could only talk about it with himself.

'We should leave it like this,' Simon said.

'So it's the same when he comes back?' Lily asked.

'Yeah.' Simon hesitated. 'Maybe . . .'

2

The sun was bright and the sea was blue. Set after set of waves rolled and crashed onto Bondi Beach. Out from the shore, a burst of spray slapped Simon's face as he moved his board into the line-up, waiting to catch the perfect peak.

At last a big wave rose, spitting chunks of white foam. Simon turned to go with it. He kicked his legs and paddled hard, clawing through the water until he caught the crest.

Simon stayed in the moment, working the wave for all it was worth until it broke. A massive wall of water crashed down on him, tearing the leash from his board.

'He's gone!'

From the southern cliff overlooking the beach, Cutler kept his binoculars focused on the foaming water.

Anderson pointed. 'There—he's up now!'

Simon's dark head bobbed in the surf, close to shore.

'He's game,' Cutler said. 'Saw the big wave and went for it.'

'And fit,' the other man added. 'Do you think he's up to the job?'

Cutler nodded. 'Time to visit the family again.'

Simon dug into the dirt and tipped a shovel-load of earth to the side of the hole. 'That should be deep enough.'

'I'm not sure I want to do this today,' Glenda said, as she placed a pot plant on the ground by the front fence. 'Maybe we can do it when Lil gets home from her drama camp.'

'She's away for a week!' Simon said. 'I thought we said we'd finish jobs around the house. Stuff left over . . . for when Dad comes back.'

'Yes, I know we did,' she said. 'But it's been four weeks, Simon.'

'This is a coffee plant,' Simon went on. 'Arabica something. The one Dad grew from a seed. Dad wants to grow it here, in the full sun. So he can make his own coffee.'

'It'll be a long time before we get a cup of coffee from this,' Glenda said, with a weak smile.

'If we don't plant it out, it'll . . . die.'

Without thinking, he had said *the word*. 'Sorry,' he mumbled.

'It's all right,' Glenda replied. 'It's something we

have to think about.' She dragged the pot closer. 'Okay, let's do it.'

'Mum? We haven't talked about Dad much,' Simon said.

'No.'

'Did Dad . . . ever say he was unhappy?' Simon groped for the right words. 'Did he say that he didn't want to be with us?'

Glenda picked a worm out of the hole and dropped it further along the garden bed. She shook her head. 'But I think he'd been worried about something. For a long time.'

'About his work?'

'He never said what, exactly. He always kept those things to himself.' She lowered the plant into the hole. 'And then there were those times he went away. You know, those business trips he went on last year. Just going. Without saying where.'

'Lil and me thought you and Dad might be busting up,' Simon said. 'But then Dad would come back and things would be sort of normal again.'

Glenda touched his arm. 'Your father and I weren't breaking up.'

'But he was feeling bad,' Simon said, 'about something.'

Glenda sighed. 'I guess we'll never know what.'

Simon looked up as a car door slammed in the street. A man stood by the car. It was Cutler. He nodded to Simon.

'Morning!' Cutler called out.

Simon stood up and moved to stand in front of his mother.

Cutler came up to the gate. 'I think that I should introduce myself properly this time. I'm Captain Rex Cutler.'

'You said you were from the government,' Simon said.

Cutler nodded towards the house. 'Perhaps we could have a chat inside?'

Simon didn't move.

'It does have something to do with your father,' Cutler added.

'It's all right, Simon,' Glenda said. 'It could be important. I was going to make a drink, anyway. Please, Captain, come inside.'

Over a cup of tea at the dining table, Simon listened as Cutler explained that he was one of a select group who had known Hale Savage well, and had worked with him on several top-secret research and development projects.

'Top secret?' Simon asked. 'Dad never talked about that.'

Glenda shook her head. 'He never even hinted at anything like that.'

'That's because he wasn't allowed to,' Cutler replied. 'And that's why we had to visit your house so quickly . . . after he was gone. In case he had left any classified information in his office.'

'Classified,' Simon muttered. 'I never knew his work was that important.'

Cutler stirred his tea. 'What I'm about to tell you is also classified, but I want to bring you into my confidence. I've come to see you today because I want you to know who I really work for, and what we might be able to do for you.' Cutler hesitated. 'Though I should warn you, this is a conversation I will deny ever took place.'

Simon tried to catch his mother's eye. He didn't know what to make of this man.

But Glenda nodded. She was giving Cutler the benefit of the doubt.

'I work for an international organisation called the Time Bureau,' Cutler said. 'You won't find us in the phone book. And we don't have a website——'

'Do you mean atomic clocks?' Simon interrupted. 'Dad was in nuclear research, wasn't he?'

'That's what I understood,' Glenda said.

'I'm afraid that was a cover story,' Cutler said. 'His field of research was more complex than that. It involved very advanced technology.'

Glenda looked warily at Cutler. 'So what do you want? Why do you want to talk with us?'

'Well, Mrs Savage, we know you're short of money.'

'You've been spying on us!' Simon said.

Cutler frowned. 'With the best of intentions.'

'I don't like this at all!' Glenda said.

'Mum's right. What do you want?'

Cutler chose his words carefully. 'Mrs Savage, the Time Bureau feels a responsibility towards your family. Both to you and your children.'

Glenda frowned. 'Are you saying you accept responsibility for my husband's disappearance?'

'No. That was totally unexpected from our point of view,' Cutler replied. 'But we do feel that Hale's disappearance might have had something to do with the pressures of his work.'

'You know that for sure?' Simon asked.

'No,' Cutler said. 'But, as I say, we feel partly responsible for the difficulties you're now having in making ends meet. He did leave you in an awkward financial situation.'

Glenda nodded. 'The house is heavily mortgaged. There's almost nothing left in my bank account.'

Simon turned to her. 'Is this true, Mum?'

'Unfortunately, yes. We're nearly broke,' she replied. 'I was planning to look for a job.'

'This is where we would like to help,' Cutler said. 'Mrs Savage, I understand your parents live in England. In Bristol?'

'That's right,' Glenda replied. 'My mother and father moved to Australia when I was young. They lived here for many years. They decided to go back to England about eighteen months ago.'

'Along with Simon and Lily, they are your closest family now,' Cutler stated.

Glenda nodded.

'What are you getting at?' Simon asked.

'I'll come to that in a moment,' Cutler replied. 'But first, I should inform you both that the Time Bureau will be holding an official enquiry into Hale's disappearance. This will be secret and out of the public eye. But, Mrs Savage, as the Bureau is based in England, it might be useful for you to be close by while we carry out this investigation.'

Glenda blinked. 'You want us to go over there?'

'At the Bureau's expense,' Cutler said. 'And, as this investigation will take some time, we would like to offer to send Lily and Simon to good schools. In addition, we'll give you a secure job in the Civil Service, a house, free moving costs, a car.'

Glenda looked thoughtful. 'You said *schools*. You mean different schools for my kids?'

'Yes,' Cutler said. 'There's a top-class day school in Bristol that would suit your daughter perfectly. It has a strong music and drama curriculum. Close to your family, too, if you chose to live there.' He looked at Simon. 'But for your son, we would suggest an elite boarding school in the Sussex Downs.'

'You're kidding!' Simon protested. 'I'm not going to some posh school!'

'It's more than that,' Cutler said. 'It's a place your father visited many times. It has first-rate scientific research facilities that he helped to develop.'

'I'm not that hot on science,' Simon said. 'Why would I want to go there?'

'You'll get a first-class education at our expense,' Cutler went on. 'And there are good sporting facilities. We put a lot of emphasis on fitness and personal training.'

Simon shrugged.

'My husband never mentioned a connection with any school,' Glenda said. She thought for a moment. 'Captain, are you serious about this?'

'I'm dead serious,' Cutler said. 'Come to England, Mrs Savage. Have a look for yourself. Then, if you're satisfied that what I am offering is above board——'

'Why are you being so generous?' Simon asked.

'Well, as I said, your father did a lot of work with the Time Bureau,' Cutler replied. 'Unique research with far-reaching effects for the future of humanity. We feel a big debt to him. You could say it's a way of repaying him for his efforts, by helping you and your family.'

'We appreciate your offer, but I'm sorry, Captain.' Glenda stood up. 'You seem dedicated, and obviously believe in what you're doing. But . . . well, for us, it's out of the question.'

She moved down the hallway to the front door. Cutler rose from the table and followed her.

'My family's gone through a lot in the last month,' Glenda went on, 'and I can't see us packing up, pulling up our roots. I can't see us moving to another country.'

'I'd like you to reconsider . . .' Cutler said.

'Mum, can I talk to you?' Simon said. He came up to Glenda and led her onto the front porch, out of Cutler's earshot. 'We can't say no.'

Glenda almost laughed. She hadn't laughed for weeks. 'Simon, this man wants us to leave everything. Send you and Lil to schools in another country. What are you talking about?'

'But Cutler's involved with this school they want to send me to,' Simon replied. 'He said Dad's work was connected with it, too. And they're going to investigate his disappearance. Maybe, if we're over there, we can find out what happened to Dad.'

Glenda frowned. 'Do you really want to know?'

'We can't live the rest of our lives just wondering.' Simon touched her arm. 'You said earlier, we might never know. But maybe we can find out *why* Dad died!'

3

Three months later, England

'This is why you are at this school,' Captain Cutler said. He swept his arm to indicate what lay before them.

Simon stepped off the metal staircase into a section of a vast circular tunnel. Ahead of them was what appeared to be a long, metal-plated pipeline, about a metre in diameter. It followed the curve of the tunnel in both directions and disappeared into darkness.

Simon looked back up the staircase. Fifteen minutes earlier, at ground level, they had walked through a hidden entrance in the side of a hill, and then through scores of rooms and chambers.

Cutler had told him these were the secret headquarters of the Time Bureau. Apparently, the Bureau employed about five hundred people, some of whom lived in the nearby towns, without their neighbours knowing their true jobs or identities. Simon hadn't been told the reason for all the secrecy.

Then they had descended the staircase until they were a hundred metres underground.

'This is why the Time Bureau exists,' Cutler went on. 'This is a section of our Time Accelerator. You've heard of the Large Hadron Collider?' he asked. 'The one on the Swiss–French border that they use for advanced physics experiments.'

'Dad showed me a picture of it in the paper,' Simon said. 'It's twenty-seven k's across, or something like that.'

'This is smaller, only one kilometre across,' Cutler explained. 'But it's as powerful as its bigger cousin.' He smiled. 'I'm not a scientist, but I can tell you this is the most essential piece of machinery that we use in our work.'

Simon stared at Cutler. 'So, if this is a Time Accelerator, what is your work?'

'I think it's time I gave you a full explanation,' Cutler said slowly. 'Simon, everyone thinks they're unique. But in your case this is true.'

'Meaning what?'

'You might have noticed that I scanned you, your sister and your mother when I first visited your house, four months ago.'

Simon nodded. 'The gadget with the blue beam.'

'It's something we do routinely,' Cutler went on. 'We scan everyone. We're authorised to do it because we're looking for something special. And only about one in ten million people have it.'

This made Simon even more curious. 'Have what?'

Cutler took the scanner from his pocket and held it in his palm. 'This simple-looking instrument is actually a sophisticated genetic testing device,' he said. 'It reads DNA and records it.'

'And you recorded ours?' Simon asked.

'We discovered that yours is particularly interesting. You have a genetic structure that is strong and flexible. That's why we invited you here. Your genetic results fit our profile. You're perfect for our program.'

'So, I'm not here just for school?' Simon said.

He thought of Mayfield Manor, the stately home built up on the surface nearby. It stood at the foot of the hill that contained the Time Bureau, and was fitted out as an exclusive boarding school. 'This isn't about improving my education?' he asked.

'Not in the way you might think,' Cutler replied. 'You're here so that we can train you. Train you as a time traveller. What we call a temponaut.'

'You want me to be a time traveller?' Simon said. 'There's no such thing.'

'We have the technology. Here's part of it, right in front of your eyes. Just around the bend to your left, there's a Travel Chamber and other equipment associated with sending our temponauts on their missions.' Cutler paused to let the information sink in. 'We regularly travel through time.'

This guy is nuts, Simon thought. 'This isn't what I

signed up for,' he said. 'I thought you were sending me to school. I don't believe in time travel. I want you to ring my mum in Bristol, and tell her to come and pick me up.'

'Are you sure?' Cutler asked.

'Yeah. I've never been more sure. I want to go home.'

'Think it through,' Cutler went on. 'If you go back to Australia, all this comes to an end. We stop supporting your mother and sister. The job, the house, the school, everything.'

Simon bristled. 'Are you threatening me?'

'On the contrary,' Cutler replied calmly, 'I'm giving you the chance to be involved in this project. One that also involved your father.'

'*This* is what Dad was working on?' Simon asked.

'Look around,' Cutler said. 'This is all a result of your father's work. This is why he got involved with the Time Bureau.'

'You mean he worked on the Time Accelerator?'

'Your father's field of research was time travel,' Cutler said. 'In fact, he did more than that. He *invented* time travel.'

Simon looked around curiously, his anger gone. 'But at the Large Hadron Collider they just work with particles,' he said. 'Are you really telling me that you can send *people* through time?'

'Yes.'

'And this time machine can send people anywhere?'

'Yes. We have this technology because of your father.' Cutler placed a hand on Simon's shoulder. 'If you stay, you'll be sent on missions through time. It's challenging work. And we want you to be part of it.'

Simon thought for a few moments. The information Cutler was giving him sounded ridiculous, but what if it were true? The events of the last few months had felt like a weird dream. Leaving Sydney, coming to the UK and arriving at this school seemed unreal. Maybe he should stay and find out where the dream would lead him next. 'I've got one question,' he said.

'Sure.'

'This investigation into Dad's disappearance,' Simon said, 'is it still on? What have you found out?'

'We've uncovered very little new information,' Cutler replied. 'But the investigation is continuing.'

So they're in no hurry, Simon thought. I'm going to have to find out for myself.

And to do that, he would have to stay close to everything associated with his father. He took a deep breath. 'Okay, Captain, don't call Mum. I'll stay.'

'Good,' Cutler replied. 'You've made the right decision.'

Simon managed a smile. Just how he would find out about his dad's disappearance, he didn't know. Not yet. But there had to be a way.

4

Spring sunshine bathed the front steps of Mayfield Manor. Simon struggled to stay awake as he sprawled on the warm stones.

He was exhausted after a morning spent learning the basics of horse riding. It was one of the activities he had chosen under the heading *Sporting Interests* on his enrolment form. And it was turning out okay. He didn't like tennis or cricket, and his top choice—surfing—was impossible in this part of the country.

His bum and legs were sore from trying to stay in the saddle. Keen to get some movement back into his body, he got to his feet and ran down the steps, into the garden. He jogged past the hedge maze, through a cluster of trees and bushes, and stopped in a clearing with a view of the Sussex Downs.

Beyond the distant hills were a few towns and villages, but the manor was isolated on its hundred hectares of parkland and forest.

It was a situation that suited its purpose perfectly, as Simon had recently discovered. From the main road, about half a kilometre away, passing motorists would see only the sign by the flint-stone gatehouse:

INSTITUTE OF ADVANCED LEARNING

INTERNATIONAL SCHOOL

FOR TALENTED STUDENTS

And, Simon thought, even if a visitor did get past the heavily guarded gates, everything would appear normal. First, they would see the mansion, the lake and the gardens. They might catch a glimpse of the rest of the grounds, which contained two training fields, a picturesque old cricket oval, tennis courts, well-equipped stables for a dozen horses, and a jogging track that weaved through a large stand of beechwood forest. If they went inside, on the ground floor of the mansion they would find a grand entrance hall, a big kitchen, two classrooms, an oak-panelled dining room, library, billiard room and a ballroom with ornate ceilings. An elaborately carved staircase led to two other floors with thirty centrally heated bedrooms. The place looked just like any other exclusive school—an ideal location for the small group of apparently well-heeled international students.

Simon smiled as he looked back over his shoulder at the hill that rose behind the mansion. There lay the true heart of Mayfield—the Time Bureau headquarters and the Time Accelerator that Simon had briefly visited. An investment that had cost worldwide governments tens of billions of dollars.

All this because of my dad, Simon thought to himself for the hundredth time. He wondered how he could have known so little about his father.

A horn beeped and a yellow minibus drove slowly up the drive. Four young faces stared through the tinted windows.

Simon made his way back through the garden to the parking area at the steps of the mansion. He had been the first student to enrol, and had spent the past week waiting impatiently for the others to arrive. Captain Cutler had explained that there could eventually be another twenty-five temponauts living here. If and when they were recruited. Finding the right kids took a lot of searching.

As the new recruits stepped from the bus, Simon wondered how many thousands, or maybe millions, of kids had been scanned to come up with this small group.

There was a skinny English-looking boy with brown spiky hair and clothes that reeked of inner-city attitude. He was joined by a tall Chinese boy with hair shaven to a number one, and a black girl with hair tied back in a ponytail. Both were more conservatively dressed than the first boy. They gazed around curiously.

The last passenger to get out was a slim, freckled,

fair-haired girl. She hesitated at the door and looked around warily. Almost as if she didn't believe her eyes.

She glanced in Simon's direction and smiled briefly.

'Hello, and welcome!' Captain Cutler's voice boomed from the top of the steps. 'There you are, Simon! Enjoy the horse ride? Come inside, all of you.'

The other kids turned, glanced at Simon and moved off.

A rare bunch of guys, Simon mused as he watched them troop up the steps. Behind him, the fair-haired girl stopped and looked around at the countryside.

'Your big chance,' Simon said jokingly. 'Now you can make a run for it!'

She didn't reply, but took a deep breath, seemed to call on some inner strength, and followed the others.

Simon waited for a moment longer. He wanted to enjoy what were probably the last minutes of his own company for a long time.

Then, unable to put it off any longer, he went inside.

5

The 24th Century, North America

The cave of the Chieftain was dimly lit with candles.

The skulls of giant alligators, sabre-toothed tigers, tusked boars and other predators decorated the rough stone walls. Their teeth and tusks were plated with gold and glinted in the smoky half-light.

A teenage boy knelt at the foot of some steps that led to a tall throne. The throne was carved from a single block of polished red granite and was occupied by a man in a white robe. The man's bare arms were tattooed with Celtic-knot motifs and his fingers were laden with heavy gold rings. His face was hidden by a hood pulled forward to the level of his eyes.

'I . . . I can't explain where she went,' the boy stammered.

'Where did you lose her, Damien?' the Chieftain growled.

'Somewhere near the castle, as we were returning.'

Damien then went on to explain how his sister, Danice, had mysteriously vanished on their latest mission. Telling the story wasn't easy. Damien was afraid of this man who sent him, and other kids, searching for gold. The Chieftain ruled their area, and could order punishment, imprisonment and death.

'When did you notice her missing?' the Chieftain asked.

'Only a few minutes from our pick-up spot,' Damien said. 'We had to go under a bridge . . .' He paused a moment to recall. 'And when I looked back, to see if she was following me—she was gone.'

'Careless boy! You should have tried to find her!' the Chieftain shouted. 'She was essential to my search for gold!'

'It was my mistake, Chieftain, I'm sorry.' Damien bowed his head lower, afraid to show any feelings for his missing sister. His family depended on the Chieftain for food and survival. It would do Damien no good to show he was more worried about Danice than he was about the Chieftain's search for gold. It was gold that kept the Chieftain in his position of power, and it was this position of power that protected Damien's family.

'Forgive me, I had no time to search,' Damien said. 'I thought it best to return and report to you.'

Damien was also reluctant to tell the Chieftain

the full story. So he didn't mention that two men had jumped out of the darkness. Or that one man had grabbed his sister, while Damien struggled with the other, before managing to break away and escape. He was afraid that the Chieftain might decide the mission was too difficult and call it off. If he did that, there would be no gold. And no gold meant no food for Damien's family.

There was a short silence before the Chieftain raised his jewelled right hand. 'I am most displeased. However, our work will go on. Did you find gold?'

'The treasure room is full of gold plate, gold bars, all sorts of gold,' Damien confirmed.

'And there are guards?'

'There are four but they are often sleepy. They drink a lot of wine.'

The Chieftain crossed his arms over his broad chest. 'You will steal the gold in two days' time. So make sure your companions are ready. Who will you take with you now?'

'My other sister—Alli,' Damien said. 'She's worked with us a few times already.'

'Yes, she's reliable,' the Chieftain replied. 'And you can take that new boy. His name?'

'His name's Lee. Yes, Chieftain, he'll make up the team.'

The Chieftain waved his hand dismissively. 'Very well, you may go.'

Damien stood, bowed and turned away. He

crossed the flagstone floor of the cave and retreated through a doorway carved out of the solid rock. He didn't look back.

For ten seconds, the chamber remained silent.

'Has he gone now, O'Bray?' the Chieftain asked. 'O'Bray, where are you!'

A thin, bald man dressed in a black robe entered the cave through the same doorway. 'Yes, boss, I heard you. He's on his way back to the Big Forest.'

'Then switch on the lights! Douse those stinking candles!'

O'Bray flicked a switch hidden inside a tiger skull. The cave filled with electric light and the Chieftain pushed back the hood of his robe. He blinked in the brightness and ran a hand through his long, straggly white hair.

'Get me some decent clothes to put on—and a strong drink!' he growled.

'Yes, boss. Right away, boss,' O'Bray replied, snuffing out the candles. The Chieftain was in one of his dark moods. It was best to obey him without question.

6

Simon entered Mayfield Manor's main classroom, slid into the nearest seat and slumped down. Green light shimmered off the walls.

'Savage, be more punctual in future,' Cutler said from the seat behind him.

Simon glanced back. 'Yeah, okay. Sorry . . . sir.' He was trying to get used to addressing senior staff as 'sir' or 'ma'am'. He didn't like it much. But the Bureau was run on semi-military lines, with much of the discipline centred on punctuality, smart manners, pressed clothes and tidy rooms; and punishments that included grubby kitchen-cleaning duties or dozens of early morning laps around the jogging track. Simon was only now remembering to make his bed every morning.

Cutler made a hushing motion and nodded to the speaker at the front of the room.

Professor McPhee was Head of the Time Bureau.

In the past few days, Simon had learnt that McPhee was in charge of the whole organisation, while Captain Cutler was responsible for its day-to-day operations.

The professor wore a crisply tailored dark suit, and had close-cropped hair and a beard that Simon imagined would be grey in normal light, but was currently a sickly green. The colour came from a hologram at the centre of the podium. It was a three-dimensional image of a temponaut—a figure nearly twice the professor's height. 'This gives you a pretty accurate look at the travel suit and equipment issued to every time traveller,' McPhee said.

Full of curiosity, Simon leaned forward. The computer-generated figure was clothed in a thick, body-conforming suit, with a helmet and faceguard. Chunky-soled shoes integrated seamlessly into the outfit. On the outside of both thighs there were zip pouches for carrying documents and small pieces of equipment.

'Of course, it is more than a suit,' McPhee said. 'Several of you have asked why we took skin and hair samples from each of you.'

There was a murmur of agreement.

'That's easily answered,' he went on. 'We took your genetic material and combined it with special fabrics and memory polymers to make a biodynamic suit that is very much like a second layer of skin. It organically becomes part of your body while you wear it. Each suit is individually made. You might say it is *grown* for you. Every time you travel you wear a new suit.'

Using a remote control, McPhee made the figure rotate. 'In addition, the suit is waterproof. It will protect you against extremes of heat and cold. The helmet can also be retracted, like this . . .'

The Professor clicked the remote and the holographic helmet retreated over the head of the figure, like liquid skin, and disappeared into the collar of the suit.

Simon glanced at the fair-haired girl who had been last off the bus. She was still looking wary, glancing continually at every person and every part of the room, and twitching and shifting in her seat, as though she didn't want to be there. Her edginess irritated him. Why had they recruited someone like her? Didn't they want people who were steady and reliable? The girl looked in his direction. Simon focused back on the professor.

'The suit also provides camouflage when you need it,' McPhee was explaining, as he brought up a pattern on the holographic figure. 'It takes on the colour and patterns of your surroundings, such as trees and foliage, even bricks and timber walls. But of course, when you travel to another time, you will often be issued with the clothing of the era to cover these suits.'

He brought the figure to a stop. 'The main feature

of your suit is this: it contains countless billions of nano-molecules that retain an exact memory of your body shape. Your size, the colour of your eyes and hair, everything. It allows us to convert your body to pure energy and transmit you across time. The nano-molecules then re-form your body at your destination. Now, any questions?'

The Chinese boy put up his hand. 'What you just said about transmitting us across time. How do we get from place to place, and from time to time?'

McPhee nodded. 'Good question. The technology is based on the Time Accelerator, of course. And the use of Time Positioning Satellites, timelines and wormholes.' He stepped closer to the front row of seats. 'You'll learn more about this during the tour of our establishment later today. But, basically, what happens is as follows: before you depart on a mission, we send a Time Positioning Satellite—or TPS— ahead of you, to open up the timeline to your exact destination. Then, you enter the Travel Chamber.'

'What we call the Spin Box,' Cutler added.

'Exactly. You enter the Spin Box,' McPhee went on. 'Your body is dematerialised and you reappear through a wormhole at your destination. Sometimes, the TPS will stay and hold the timeline open. At other times, it will depart, and return to fetch you at a pre-programmed time. Understood?'

'Yes, Professor,' the voices murmured around the room.

'Any other questions?' McPhee asked.

The black girl shifted in her seat. 'So, sir, why do you use kids as temponauts?' she asked in a clear voice with an American accent. 'Why not use adults?'

'We have used adults until now, mainly volunteer soldiers,' McPhee replied, 'but we get only nine, maybe ten missions out of them before health issues start to become a problem. We need people who can go on many time-trips. Temponauts who are aged between eleven and fifteen, and who weigh under forty-five kilos, are best. The lighter you are, the easier it is to dematerialise and rematerialise your body and send it through time.' He held his arms out. 'We adults are too big. After ten or so missions, it's dangerous for us. The body starts to change, to age and to deteriorate. This is not the case with children.'

Simon raised his hand. 'Nice threads, Prof—but how do you take a leak?'

A burst of laughter swept the room and McPhee allowed himself a smile. 'Well, that's right to the point. Astronauts are often asked that sort of question.' He paused. 'The suit has a built-in feature that allows you to release the fabric around key areas of your body. Don't worry, full instructions are provided. Satisfied?'

The students nodded and grinned at each other.

'Anyway, I know you'll have other questions just as, ah, fascinating as that one,' McPhee said, 'and we can answer them during the tour of our facilities.' He clicked the remote, the hologram disappeared and fluorescent light filled the room.

'Something else to think about,' McPhee added, lifting a hand to scratch the beard that was, indeed, grey. 'Just as importantly, you will be learning a couple of interesting things about time travel. One, that it is not only the present that is real, but the past and the future, too.' McPhee peered thoughtfully at the group. 'Secondly, that what you can do today, you can also do yesterday and tomorrow.'

There were murmurs of incomprehension around the room.

'That's deep!'

'What's that mean?'

'Beats me.'

'Okay, that's all!' the professor said. 'Just one further instruction. Don't forget to fill out your Training Request Forms. You can ask for additional training in any area of our operations that interests you personally. Is that clear?'

'Yes, Professor,' everyone replied.

'Right, that is all for the present. You can spend a few minutes introducing yourselves, then we go on our tour,' the professor said. 'We'll start at the front steps. See you there in ten minutes.'

As Simon left his chair, he was bumped aside by the spiky-haired boy. He seemed in a hurry to get to the door first.

'Watch it, sport!' The boy grinned. 'Don't get in my way!'

'Watch it yourself!' Simon retorted.

'That's Nick Spenser,' a voice said beside him.

Simon turned to the tall Chinese boy.

'I'm Ivan Ho,' the boy said. 'This is Taylor Bly,' he added, introducing the American girl.

'They reckon we'll all get together and socialise a bit later,' Taylor said, 'but most of us got to know each other on the bus already. This time-travel stuff is crazy, isn't it!'

'Excuse me, Savage,' Cutler interrupted, ushering Simon aside. 'There is someone we want you to get to know. Right away.'

Why is Cutler singling me out? Simon wondered.

The fair-haired girl sprang to her feet.

'Hi, Simon,' she said, pushing out a hand to greet him. 'I'm Danice.'

Simon shook her hand. He was surprised by her firm grip. She was easily ten centimetres shorter than he was but, up close, he could see she was wiry and had muscular arms and shoulders. 'So, where are you from?' he asked.

Danice glanced uncertainly at the professor.

'Danice is from a long way away,' McPhee said smoothly.

'Actually, she's from another time altogether,' Cutler added.

'We hope you two will get to know each other,' McPhee said.

'So, how did they find you?' Simon asked Danice.

Danice looked at the professor again, once more unsure of how to answer.

They recruit all kinds here! Simon thought to himself.

'We did a deal with Danice to enable her to work here,' Cutler said. 'You don't need to know any more.'

Simon glanced at Danice, but her closed expression told him nothing. He turned to the professor. 'Do you want me to show her around?'

'More than that,' McPhee replied. 'From today, you two will work together. She's your partner.'

Simon felt a moment of confusion. Where had this partner idea come from? 'Sir, that's not what you told me at my first interview. You said we worked alone.'

'I think I said that we'd train you to be self-sufficient and resourceful,' Cutler replied.

'Big words that mean whatever you want them to mean,' Simon muttered under his breath.

He didn't want to hang out with Danice, especially not in his free time. He had things to find out. He didn't know how, but he wanted to see if he could uncover a few clues about his father's death.

'Savage, learn this now,' McPhee said. 'In this job,

new situations come up all the time and we have to deal with them. We have a special mission coming up. As a result, you two will work together.'

'We have new plans for you,' Cutler added. 'You had better get used to it.'

Simon glanced at Danice. 'You mean, new plans since you recruited me?' he asked.

'Something like that,' Cutler said.

Simon sighed. Danice was a complication he hadn't anticipated. And he didn't like it, not one bit.

Simon woke from a restless sleep. He sat up and stared for a moment into the dark corners of his room. He'd been dreaming of tunnels and wormholes, when suddenly an idea had formed. A new plan to find out more about his father.

On their tour the previous afternoon, the tempo-nauts had glimpsed the Time Bureau's Command Centre through an observation window. Captain Cutler had explained that the centre controlled every time-travel mission, and stored all the Bureau's operational information in its computers.

I have to get into the Command Centre, Simon thought.

When he filled out his Training Request Form, he would ask for instruction in the Time Control and Mission Tracking System. This would get him past the strict security and into the Command Centre. Once inside, he might be able to discover what information the Bureau had about his father. It was worth a try.

He rested his head back on the pillow and closed his eyes.

7

The yowl of a wild animal cut through the dusk. Damien stood rigid at the edge of the forest.

This was the danger period: the shadowy, early evening when animals awoke from their sleep and began their nocturnal prowl. Damien had to be extra careful in these twilight hours, and for a few moments he thought of retracing his steps back to the safety of the Chieftain's fortress on the cliff top. The buildings, lookouts, landing tower and grounds were surrounded by a high stone wall. And so were the series of caves beneath them. If Damien wanted, he could scrounge a blanket and sleep in the safety of the compound, and then return to his family in the morning. But he had to get home right away. He had to tell them about Danice. Although he didn't want to think about how he would break the news.

The howl rose through the trees again, now more distant. Whatever the creature was, it was moving away. It presented no immediate threat but, all the same, Damien turned sharply and headed back towards the cliffs. It would be safer to take the Uptrack. This was a higher path, about halfway up the cliff face, and it was a longer way home. But it was less dangerous than the direct route through the darkening forest.

He reached the first piles of mossy boulders at the base of the cliffs and started to climb.

'Damien! Damien!'

He looked up to see his younger sister, Alli, staring down at him from the Uptrack.

Damien scrambled up the last of the scree. 'What are you doing here?'

'It's late, we were getting worried,' Alli said, pushing strands of straggly dark hair out of her eyes. 'Mama guessed you might avoid the wildlings and come this way.' She looked around. 'Where's Danice?'

'She's not . . . with me.' Damien suddenly felt a deep shame for having lost their sister. He lowered his eyes. 'They . . . they took her!'

Alli gripped his arm. 'Who took her?'

'I don't know! Everything was going fine . . .'

Suddenly the story came pouring out. 'We were heading back to our timeline, to return here,' Damien said. 'We were almost there when these two guys jumped out.' He glanced at Alli. 'They were wearing time-travel suits. Not like the ones we wear, but better.'

'What—you're saying they were time-trippers too?' Alli said.

'Yes. They had to be,' Damien said. 'One of the guys grabbed Danice and pushed her into a wormhole. A different one. Not ours. I hadn't even noticed it was there. One minute she was with me, the next she was gone.'

'What did you do?'

'What could I do?' Damien said. 'The other guy grabbed me . . . I struggled with him. I kicked him back against a tree, and kind of stunned him . . . then . . . I just ran off. I was scared.' Damien hung his head. 'I'm sorry, Alli, I'm really sorry.'

'What's the Chieftain doing about it?' Alli asked.

'Nothing,' Damien said.

'What did you tell him?'

'Not much,' Damien said. 'I didn't dare. You know what he's like. He doesn't care about us.'

'But what can we do about Danice?' Alli demanded.

'Nothing. We can't get to the Chieftain's Time Accelerator. And we don't know how to operate it. Only the Chieftain and O'Bray can do that.'

'So we don't know who took her, and we don't know where she's gone,' Alli said.

'She's gone to . . . some other time.'

'And we can't search for her.'

Damien shook his head. 'No. She could be anywhere in time.'

'We have to tell Mama.'

'I know . . . I know,' Damien murmured.

Alli struggled not to cry as the news sank in. With Danice gone, Damien would need her help. She had to stay strong and focused, and hold back her tears for when she was alone. 'Come on, it's almost dark,' she said. 'We'd better get home.'

Damien followed her. The narrow track rose steeply in front of them and they climbed in silence until they were above the forest. Beneath their feet the giant redwood canopy stretched like a vast green carpet to the distant horizon. According to stories, it took forty days on foot to reach the Far Lands on the other side, although no one in living memory had tried it. There were too many hazards to make such a journey worthwhile.

'Alli?'

'What?'

'I didn't tell you—we're making another trip, in two days' time.'

'We lose our sister—and we still have to keep going on trips!' Alli protested. 'How much gold does that greedy old guy want?'

'*Shusssh!*' Damien hissed, even though there was no one around to hear them.

'Yeah, the birds might hear and tell on us,' Alli said.

'Well, what choice do we have?' Damien asked bitterly. 'We don't want to end up like Bigdad.' He glanced back in the direction of Old City, north of the Chieftain's fortress. 'It's no fun being a slave and working for the Tribunes in their factories. Those evil old men are the real rulers of this land, not the Chieftain.'

'That's true, but it's no fun getting kidnapped by people from another time, either. How many more trips will we have to make before the Chieftain's happy?'

Damien shrugged. 'Who knows? These Spanish guys I saw today took mountains of gold from some New World. The Chieftain says there's a lot.'

'And he'll make us steal every last piece of it, I reckon,' Alli said, as they reached the point where the path dropped back towards the gloomy forest below.

'Come on—we'd better run!' Damien said.

He ran down the slope, between a stand of towering redwoods, and was first into the clearing beyond. The last rays of the sun lit the very top branches of two massive trees in the clearing. Their ancient trunks had fused together at the base to form a colossal column a hundred metres high.

Damien reached into a hole in the trunk's fibrous bark and took out a short wooden club.

'Hurry ... hurry ... up!' Alli puffed, glancing fearfully over her shoulder.

Damien took a step away from the base of the tree and bent down to a small, hollow log which had been stripped of its bark. He drummed on the log three times, then waited and tapped it another three times.

After a moment, a long rope ladder tumbled down the trunk. It swung wildly as the bottom rung reached the ground. Damien yanked at the ladder until it was tight and even.

'Best to tell Mama the news straightaway,' Alli said, grabbing the bottom rung.

'I will. But how do you reckon she'll take it?'

'With Dad gone, and now Danice?' Alli replied. 'Badly.'

Damien nodded. 'You first!'

Alli started to climb.

The frightened whoop of a bird echoed sharply through the clearing. Damien spun around. The bushes rustled a short distance away.

Damien leapt onto the ladder and followed his sister up into the thick green canopy of branches.

8

The year 2000, New York City

Simon was getting annoyed. He was also getting worried.

He stood by the news stand with a copy of the latest issue of *The New Yorker* magazine rolled up and inserted into the pouch on the right thigh of his travel suit. That part of his first mission was completed and on schedule. Now all he had to do was meet up with Danice, then return to their timeline in a quiet alley near Grand Central Station. They were supposed to have met five minutes previously. Simon stepped out from the side of the stand and looked up and down the street. Cars, trucks and yellow cabs beeped loudly and crowds of office workers scurried along the pavements.

'So, buddy, where's your bike?' the news vendor asked.

Simon looked away. He was supposed to be inconspicuous! He'd told the man he was a bicycle courier. This was the explanation he had been ordered to give to anyone who asked. With his helmet retracted, and a big T-shirt over the top part of his time-travel suit, he looked like any of the couriers who buzzed around the city.

'It's over the road,' Simon lied. 'I'm just waiting for a friend.'

The man turned to a new customer and Simon breathed a sigh of relief. He checked his wrist pilot, pressing a finger to the touch screen and activating a series of yellow grids. A red locator dot and a set of figures flashed in the right-hand corner. They indicated the timeline would stay open for another seven minutes, which meant that in two minutes he would have to go back alone. He wasn't crazy about the thought of reporting: *'Sorry, sir, got one magazine, lost one time traveller!'*

'So, Simon, what are we waiting for?' a voice said. It was Danice, wearing a bright-red coat over her travel suit.

'What took you so long?' Simon demanded.

'I had to find the right clothes,' she replied. 'A woman from the Bureau took me shopping a couple of times. But this was my first go by myself.'

'How could you afford that? How much did they give you?'

Danice shrugged. 'Two hundred dollars.'

'They only gave me five!' Simon held out a couple

of coins. 'And I was ordered to bring back the change.'

'I need modern clothes,' Danice replied.

'Because you're so old-fashioned?' Simon asked. 'Maybe you could tell me what era you *are* from?'

The day before, Simon and Danice had spent several hours in the underground zone that housed the Time Accelerator, learning about its basic operations. He had still discovered nothing more about her, except detecting that she had a slight American accent. But she wouldn't tell him what year she was from, or even what country she was from. And Captain Cutler was keeping them busy with a tough exercise regime, information briefings, and training missions. Simon had been unable to get away from Danice for even a minute. He was starting to feel claustrophobic.

'I can't tell you what era I'm from, you know that,' Danice said, checking her wrist pilot. 'Come on, time's up.'

Simon headed for the alley where the timeline was waiting for them. 'It's not me who's been holding us up!' he muttered.

9

Simon stepped through the airtight lock.

'Stop there!' snapped the Security Officer. 'Stop at the yellow line and remain stationary!'

Simon looked down at his bare feet and halted by the line on the floor. A series of rapidly moving red and violet beams scanned his body from head to toe.

The last couple of hours had been both weird and gross, as his time-travel suit was dissolved and peeled off his body. Now all he wanted to do was go to his room to chill out, watch TV, have a bite to eat and sleep.

'So, find any bugs?' Simon asked.

'Just checking you don't bring back any micro-organisms, bacteria, viruses or insects from the time-zone you visited,' the officer drawled.

'Yeah! I read the manual. Sir.'

'Now for your identity check.'

'I am me,' Simon murmured. He was starting to

get irritated. His first trip had been more exhausting than he could have imagined.

'Haven't heard that one before,' the officer said. 'Just place yourself at the recognition scanner.'

Simon positioned his head in front of an oval screen. There was a quick click and a flash of green light.

'And you'd better get used to this. This procedure happens every time you come back.'

Simon yawned and nodded.

The officer glared. 'And how about handing in the magazine you purchased.'

'Sure.' Simon took *The New Yorker* from the pocket of his tracksuit pants and dropped it on the counter. 'Delivered, as ordered. Sir.'

'Anything else to declare?'

Simon shook his head.

'The *coins*,' the man said, nodding towards Simon's left hand. 'I picked them up on the scanner.'

'Oh, those.' Simon plonked the coins next to the magazine.

'And your other equipment?'

'All left in the safety locker outside the Spin Box,' he replied.

'Right you are, Savage, carry on.'

'Sir!' Simon said, and strolled through the next door and into the change room.

'*Whew!*' he sighed, letting down his guard for the first time in twelve hours. Now was his official

Down Time, a rest period of seventy-two hours that would allow his body to recover its normal molecular structure after the stresses of time travel.

Simon stopped in front of the mirror. He knew there might be some bodily changes as a result of the journey, and he quickly glanced into the glass.

His hair was now a brown tangle instead of straight, his eyes seemed brighter blue, his skin a shade paler. There were blotches of red on his face and neck.

'You look a real mess,' he mumbled.

A shiny steel drink robot came gliding noiselessly alongside. It fixed its digital eye squarely on Simon's face. 'Hi, Si, care for a drink?'

'Thanks, Servo,' Simon replied, grabbing a fresh towel from the bench. A hot shower and a few laps of the pool and his body might start to get back on track.

'I've got orange and lemon, cranberry, yodelberry and tropical mix,' Servo rattled off. 'Or try our new vitamin-enriched, creamy yoghurt cola!'

'*Urgh!* No thanks! The orange and lemon'll be fine.'

There was a whirring inside the drinkbot and a small door slid open. A stainless-steel arm extended and held out a glass of frothy, freshly squeezed juice.

'Thanks,' Simon said. He was already used to speaking to robots. They carried out many basic duties in the Bureau, and were so interactive that it was easy to forget they were machines.

'A pleasure,' Servo replied. 'I hope you had a fruitful mission, too.'

'The first of many, I suppose,' Simon said, 'but nothing to boast about.'

His muscles still felt tingly and his skin itched.

Ivan Ho burst into the change room. 'Hi, Simon, how've you been?'

'Okay,' Simon replied.

'Man, how do you feel about this time-travel kick—amazing, eh?' Ivan asked. 'Feels like you're being pulled at a zillion k's an hour into a tube of glue.'

Simon nodded. 'Then that kind of explosion. Bright red and yellow light. Then . . .'

'Then nothing . . . and you wake up wherever they sent you. It's a trip, all right,' Ivan said with a broad smile. 'So, where have y*ou* been today?'

'New York, year 2000,' Simon replied. 'You?'

'Beijing, 1900. They wanted me to get some original documents on the Boxer Rebellion.'

'So, why *were* they refusing to wear underwear?'

Ivan frowned. 'The Boxers were a secret Chinese society . . .'

'I know! I know!' Simon laughed, despite his tiredness. 'They were opposing Westerners who were trying to extend their influence in the country. I read about it the other day. Major effort.'

Ivan grinned again. 'Hey, if you don't learn something in this job, what's it worth, eh?' He sat down. 'And what's with Danice? The mystery girl. You're hanging out with her, so fill us in.'

'She's under wraps. I don't know much.' Simon shrugged. 'She's a mystery all right. No one's told me anything.'

'Savage!' Cutler's voice boomed through a speaker built into the frame of the drinkbot.

'Yes, sir!'

'I want you to report to the professor,' Cutler said. 'Fifteen minutes. You can rest later.'

'Yes, sir.'

'What's that all about?' Ivan asked.

'Beats me,' Simon said, searching his locker.

Whenever Cutler wants something, it usually means trouble, he thought. Then he pushed the idea from his mind.

'Hey, have you seen my sandwich?' he asked.

Ivan laughed. 'Nick took it to Egypt, 1798.'

'Hope the Egyptians like cheese and tomato,' Simon replied, making for the door.

10

The 16th Century, Spain

A pinpoint appeared in the darkness, like the first stab of starlight in a night sky.

A second later, it grew to the size of a bottle top. Then it burst into bright yellow-and-white swirls that filled the stone-walled cellar with rippling light. The light flared off the piles of gold plate, gold bars, candlesticks, jewellery and chests of ducats. A final, brilliant flash brought a TPS spinning into the space, punching a wormhole in the air. Shadowy forms flickered far back along the time tunnel. Then suddenly they materialised in the chamber as three shimmering human forms.

A moment later they assumed their full solidity.

'*Phew*, right on target!' Damien said, shaking his body to get his limbs moving again. 'You all okay?'

Alli nodded, opening a thigh pouch on her travel suit. It was a simple but practical outfit made of a plastic-like material. She took out a hand-pump spray bottle. 'Doesn't get any easier, no matter how many times we do it. You okay, Lee?'

'Yeah, I'm okay,' a bony, red-haired boy replied. He squinted in the dank and unfamiliar surroundings. 'Are we in the right place?'

'This is it,' Damien confirmed.

'There's that bird again!' Alli pointed to a solid gold statue in the alcove above the door. It was the size of a small dog, with the head and wings of an eagle and the claws and body of a lion.

'What is it?' Lee asked. 'It's creepy.'

Damien glanced up. 'Yeah, plug ugly. It's a griffin. You see them in a lot of these places. They're an ancient sort of charm that guards the treasure.'

'Doesn't seem to work,' Alli grinned.

'Not with us around. You know what to do, Lee?' Damien reached into his own leg pouch and took out a spray bottle, then picked up a fifteen-centimetre gold bar from a stack. 'Gold bars first . . .'

'Finger bars are the most valuable,' Alli added as she covered the bar with nano-spray and tossed it into the wormhole. 'As many as you can, quick as you can.'

'And this works?' Lee asked, taking a bottle from his own pouch.

'Sure,' Alli replied. 'A squirt of this stuff sends the gold through time and pops it back into its original form at the other end.'

'Like us, when we get back?'

'Yep. That's how it works.'

'This hole's only open for fifteen minutes,' Damien said. He checked the position of the spinning TPS, which now emitted a bluish gleam that gave them enough light to work by.

'Damien, that sound, can you hear it?' Alli asked, nodding towards the solid wooden door at the end of the cellar.

'Keep working. I'll check.'

There were clinks of gold against gold as Alli and Lee lifted, sprayed and tossed the gold bars.

'They're heavy,' Lee said.

'We haven't even started!' Alli replied. She glanced at her brother. 'You hear anything?'

Damien pressed his ear against the door. 'The guards are belting out some sort of song.'

'Hopefully they won't hear us, then!'

For the next five minutes they sweated hard, tossing bar after bar into the swirling vortex.

'Lee, we're doing all right here,' Alli said, looking at the gold ornaments stacked around the repository. 'Must be dozens of those candlesticks. Grab a few!'

'The Tribunes in Old City love those,' Damien said. 'The Chieftain buys his favours with stuff like that.'

Lee crossed to a shelf which ran along one wall of the cellar. A dozen gold candlesticks stood in a gleaming row. He grabbed for the first one.

'Weighs a ton!' he exclaimed. *'Oops!'*

The heavy candlestick slipped from his sweaty grip and fell against the next one. The whole row toppled over with a resounding crash.

'Sorry!' Lee said lamely.

There were shouts from beyond the door.

'That's wrecked it!' Damien hissed. 'I'll distract the guards while you two get going!'

Alli grabbed Lee. 'You first. Move!' She gave him a shove and he was sucked into the wormhole.

Keys rattled on the far side of the door.

Damien turned to Alli. 'Get out—quick! I'll be right after you!'

'Don't wait around!' Alli yelled as she jumped into the wormhole and vanished.

Damien heard the metal bolts being thrown back. He dashed for the wormhole as the door swung open. A guard stormed in and fired his musket wildly. The round of shot tore into a wooden beam in the ceiling.

'*Adiós, amigos!*' Damien cried, leaping into the time tunnel. He hoped the gold would please the Chieftain.

The TPS spun for a second and its light swirled around the chamber. Then it was gone and the wormhole closed.

The guards gasped and sank to their knees.

'*El diablo, el diablo!*' one of them cried.

It was his only explanation for a phenomenon he would never understand.

11

'**G**ood to see you, Savage,' McPhee said, glancing away from the Timeline Operations Screen that dominated the Command Centre.

For most of Simon's stay at the manor the centre had been the Forbidden Zone. No entry, no surprise drop-in visits, nothing without security clearance. On their first guided tour, the temponauts had merely glimpsed the centre through a thick barrier of armoured glass from the neighbouring viewing room.

Now Simon was close enough to take in every detail. He stood by the command console, where an Operations Officer was permanently on duty, keeping a close watch on movements across time. The screen was about six metres by three and showed a series of coloured bands. There were twenty vertical lines indicating blocks of one century each, dating back two thousand years from Present Time, and four bands going forward four hundred years. Horizontally, two broader, yellow lines showed current missions. Nick Spenser was still in the year 1798, and Taylor Bly was in 1900.

Simon felt a shiver of anticipation. This is where I want to be, he thought. Mission Control. This is where I can find out what I need to know.

'Any sight of Spenser yet, Harry?' McPhee asked the Operations Officer, a chubby, red-faced man in an army uniform.

'No, sir,' Harry replied, 'but the timeline's just opened again. We're getting some vision of the area and he's due back to his pick-up location in ten minutes.'

'Very well, keep an eye out.' McPhee turned to Simon. 'You know how it all works?'

'Not exactly, Professor.'

'I was looking at your Training Request Form. You said that you wanted to learn how the Time Control and Mission Tracking System operates. Any special reason?'

Yes, Simon felt like saying, I want to find out how and why my dad died. But it would be stupid to tell it straight like that. 'I'm just interested,' he said.

McPhee gave Simon a searching stare before replying. 'Well, we've decided to grant your request. But for one reason only. You remember that I mentioned a special mission with Danice?'

Simon nodded.

'Good. Understanding how this system operates will help you with that,' McPhee said. 'Harry here is our rostered Operations Officer. He will give you some basic training.'

Harry twisted around on his chair. 'Harry Hammil,' he said cheerfully. 'Got any questions, just ask.'

Simon fixed his eyes back on the Operations Screen. 'Okay,' he said. 'Why do we go back in time and take documents and investigate all these different eras?'

Harry looked at McPhee. 'Would you like to take that one, sir?'

'One of our jobs is research,' McPhee explained. 'Recently, we formed a History Unit. We're rewriting some of the history of Europe, America, China and parts of Africa using original documents and facts gathered by our temponauts.'

Simon's attention switched to the future end of the screen.

'I see you're also interested in the centuries ahead,' McPhee observed, following Simon's gaze.

'Those bands going forward four centuries,' Simon said. 'Why are they there? In our training manual it says that there is some law, some regulation, about not travelling to the future. Is that right, sir?'

McPhee sat on the edge of Harry's desk. 'You're referring to a decision that was made some time ago. When time-travel technology was still in development. We thought it would be unwise for the human race to know too much of what might happen in the future.'

Simon nodded.

'If people had easy access to travelling forwards in time, they could find out things like winning lottery numbers, or the best shares to buy on the stock exchange,' McPhee went on. 'They could come back, buy tickets in the lottery, or put bets on the right horses, and make a lot of money. Unscrupulous people could use the same means to change and manipulate world events. It could be catastrophic.'

Simon nodded again. Not that long ago, he would have thought it kind of cool to know who all the future World Surfing Champions would be, and whether he'd have any chance at the title. But he had other things on his mind now.

'Take another look at the screen. A closer look,' McPhee said. 'Bring up the future timelines, Harry.'

Harry punched some keys, and six horizontal red lines appeared from a line marking the year 2321. They connected back to several vertical lines in a block eight hundred years earlier.

Simon studied them. 'They look like mission lines to a spot in the twenty-fourth century. I don't get it, sir. How does this fit in with not doing missions to the future?'

'Those are red lines, not yellow, Savage,' McPhee said. 'If you look carefully, you'll see these missions originate in the year 2321, and link to a variety of locations and times back in the sixteenth century.'

'So those aren't our missions?' Simon asked. He could think of only one other explanation. 'Does this mean someone else has worked out a time-travel system?'

Harry smiled. 'The kid's twigged straightaway, sir.'

'An organisation in the twenty-fourth century does have time-travel capability,' McPhee said, 'and the Bureau would like to find out who they are. We've got some idea of what they're up to, but we don't want this technology to fall into the wrong hands, or to be used for the wrong purposes. We want to control it.' He paused. 'And this means that the future is now part of your job.'

Simon couldn't believe his luck. He was breaking new ground. The Bureau was sending him on a mission of the utmost importance. And the more they trusted him with assignments like this, the more chances he would get to look into the past. And that way, Simon figured, he was bound to discover more about his father's disappearance.

But the past can wait a little longer, he thought to himself.

'So, how does Danice come into it, sir?' Simon asked.

'Danice lives in the twenty-fourth century,' McPhee replied. 'We brought her here to work with you—and to take you there.'

Simon was amazed. No wonder Danice had

been acting weird. She must have been even more homesick than the rest of them. 'Now I understand the secrecy,' he managed to say.

'Are you ready for it?' asked McPhee.

'Can't be soon enough for me,' Simon replied with a grin. 'Sir!'

12

Early 17th Century, England

It was market day in Bucklechurch. A few tattered flags fluttered from the battlements of the ancient castle on the hill above the town.

'This joint has seen better times,' Simon said. He and Danice left a laneway beside a ruined abbey and strolled into the town's cobblestoned square. A few dozen raggedly dressed townsfolk milled about, gawping at items that were displayed along a ramshackle row of stalls.

'That abbey was plundered by the soldiers of Henry VIII,' Danice said, pulling her hooded cloak tighter around her shoulders. 'In 1534 all the town's privileges were taken away and the local lord's title was abolished.'

'Yeah, that long ago?'

'You read the briefing file, didn't you?'

'I had a quick look at it.'

Danice grabbed Simon's arm and pulled him into a gap behind a hay-laden cart. 'You should have read it all,' she said with quiet intensity. 'These are real people, and the past is real, just like the professor said. We can't just rush in and do what we like, as if it were a game.'

Simon sighed. Danice was getting on his nerves. He'd been feeling a bit more friendly towards her since he'd discovered she was from the twenty-fourth century, but she was still a pain. Always wanting to do everything by the book. 'Look, I read our mission statement,' he said. 'This is a training run.' He looked around at the market stalls. 'We arrive, we retrieve, we leave. Stop making such a big deal of it!'

'Okay, have it your way. You take charge.'

'Good,' Simon said, heading towards the market stalls. He was frustrated that McPhee had chosen to send them to the past again, after all the big talk of going to the future. The professor had insisted on more training, and in the seventeenth century, to boot. It was a waste of time. 'Let's do what we have to,' he said, 'and get out of here.'

'The vision's dropped out from our satellite,' Harry Hammil said, swivelling in his chair to face the professor and Captain Cutler.

'Where are they now?' Cutler asked.

'They'll be entering the market,' Harry replied. 'Shall I move the TPS and the timeline?'

Cutler lifted a questioning eyebrow. 'What do you think, Professor? Are they up to the challenge?'

'Yes, move it,' McPhee ordered without hesitation. 'It's time to make things harder for them. See how they respond.'

As they sauntered past the market stalls, Simon tightened the hood of his cloak around his face to better conceal his sun-tanned skin. He and Danice wore woollen shirts and baggy breeches over their travel suits to blend in with the local townsfolk.

The Bureau's Costume Department has got it pretty right, Simon thought. But nothing prepared him for the sights and stinks of the market. The pages of their brief had been clean, but the real streets of history were far from it. The butcher's stall was a good example. The sheep carcasses hung from hooks, black flies crawling over their fatty flesh, while under the counter two mangy dogs fought over the eyeless, decaying head of a pig. Piles of garbage and grey cesspools of muck lay scattered about the square.

'Fresh mutton, young'uns?' the butcher asked, holding up a blood-spattered meat cleaver.

Danice turned away.

'Let's try over there,' Simon said, pointing to a

cookware stall heaped with bowls and cast-iron pots and pans.

Their task was to take back some solid object, and that was as good a place to look as any.

'Okay, give it a try,' Danice said.

As she turned, a burly farm boy balancing a rusty hoe on his shoulder bumped into her.

'Sorry!' Danice gasped. 'I didn't see you!'

The flaxen-haired youth scowled and stared at Danice suspiciously. He had heard rumours, only that day, that witches had been seen over the last couple of nights. Hags in disguise who had left the dark forests to haunt the villages. And now there were two cloaked and hooded strangers in the marketplace.

'Quick!' Simon grabbed Danice's elbow and steered her across to the kitchen stall.

'A good day to ye!' said the owner.

He wore a filthy leather apron, and beamed with a toothless grin as he waved a claw-like hand over his homemade range of products. 'Pray look at some of me proper fine wares. I'll make fair trade, I'll not deceive or cog thee.'

'I think he's giving us the big sell,' Danice whispered.

Simon picked up a small iron pot and turned it over in his hands. 'Well, let's nab some piece of junk, pronto,' he whispered back.

'Ah, good sir, there be a fine pot,' the fellow said.

'Yeah, a saucepan,' Simon agreed.

'Simon!' Danice snapped.

'What dost thou call it?' the man asked.

'A saucepan,' Simon said.

'Simon, shut up!' Danice hastily dropped a couple of silver coins into the man's hand. 'There, thank 'ee!'

The man's eyes popped with delight at her generosity and the spit dribbled from his lips. It was a payment three times the normal price. 'Well, thank 'ee and good bounty be with thee!'

'Let's go!' said Danice as she dragged Simon away.

'What's up?'

'You called it a saucepan!'

'That's what it is,' he replied, stashing the pot in his nano-carrier backpack.

'Not yet, it's not.'

'What?'

'It's what I was saying. We have to respect the time we're in,' Danice said, pushing through the crowd. 'The word *saucepan* wasn't used round here for another sixty years or more. Maybe not even till the eighteenth century.'

Danice was right, but Simon didn't want to admit it. 'Oh, is that all?' he said.

'It's careless,' Danice said. 'It's interfering with history.'

He stopped. 'Look, I didn't have time to check the language recordings. So I'm sorry, okay!'

On the far side of the square, the farm boy was talking with three older men and pointing towards the two temponauts. One of the men looked official. He wore an armoured breastplate, and a sword hung at his side.

'We're being watched!' Simon muttered.

Danice glanced across the square. At that moment, the boy and the men started shouting and shoving their way towards them. Attracted by the excitement, a motley rabble of townsfolk grabbed hold of makeshift weapons and joined them.

'We'd better make tracks!' Simon said, activating his wrist pilot and heading back to the laneway beside the abbey. The timeline that would take them home was at the far end of the lane, out of sight of the square.

Suddenly he stopped. 'Hang on! Where's the timeline? It's moved. Check your reading.'

Danice activated her wrist pilot. 'You're right. Now it's by the bridge on the far side of the castle. Command has shifted it!'

Simon glanced over his shoulder. The farm boy and the growing mob were now shouting, 'Witches! Witches!'

'Quick! Down here!' Simon said.

They ducked into another laneway that led out of the village to the farmlands beyond. Simon took off his cloak.

'If we get these rags off, we can use our suits

as camouflage,' he said, glancing towards the ivy-covered wall that ran alongside the laneway. 'Toss your stuff along the path. Now!'

Danice scattered her clothes along the lane as she ran. 'But we're supposed to take these costumes back with us,' she said.

'Too bad,' Simon said, as the voices of the mob got closer. 'Stand still. And stay still!'

They pressed their bodies against the wall. Within a few moments their suits took on a leaf pattern that exactly matched the ivy-covered wall. A second later, a score of angry villagers poured into the lane.

Simon and Danice froze.

'Ho, there! Look!' The farm boy pointed at the clothing. 'The witches have fled this way!'

'Advance!' the soldier ordered.

He lumbered along the lane and the crowd followed him, yelling and waving their hoes, axes and pitchforks.

Danice stepped away from the wall. 'Hey, these suits really work!'

'Yeah, but let's not stand around admiring them.' Simon grabbed her arm. 'Let's move!'

Danice tugged away from him. 'We can't run through the village in these outfits!'

She was right. Simon selected a map of the area on his wrist pilot. 'The bridge is on the other side of the castle. But we don't have to go through the square to get there.'

He glanced at the wall behind them. 'It's only a couple of metres high,' he said. 'We can climb over here. The map shows an orchard on the other side that extends around the back of the castle. After that there's a stream we can follow down to the bridge. Okay?'

'Okay!' Danice replied.

Simon took a step back, jumped and grabbed the top of the wall. 'Give us a leg-up!'

Danice crouched, cupped her hands under Simon's left foot and lifted. He straddled the wall and stretched an arm down to her. 'Grab hold—quick!'

Danice took his hand, scrambled her feet up the wall and made it to the top.

'Go!' Simon said.

Danice dropped down the other side. Simon looked around for a moment to check no one was following.

Then he, too, was gone.

13

The feast that Damien spread on the family table was the best they had seen for a month or more. There were the usual beige, tasteless chunks of Syn-food, a processed protein from the Prison Farms. But there was also a roast chicken, two loaves of fresh bread, a bunch of celery, some potatoes, carrots, apples and a big, spiky pineapple, all from the Chieftain's own private farm and kitchen.

'The Chieftain was pleased with our haul,' Damien said. 'This is our reward.'

Alli polished an apple and passed it to her mother, Hanna.

Hanna irritably waved it away. 'So, how much gold did you steal?'

'Five or six hundred kilos,' Damien replied. 'We would've got more . . . well, if Lee hadn't messed things up.'

'It was his first trip,' Alli said in Lee's defence.

'He was clumsy.'

'He'll get better.'

'He's your friend, so of course you'll defend him. But he'll have to shape up quick,' Damien said. 'These trips aren't games. They're hard work, they're dangerous——'

'Danice should be here to enjoy this, too,' Hanna cut in.

'I know Mama,' Damien replied. 'I said I was sorry about what happened.' The feast couldn't make up for his sister's disappearance, and there was no way he could start a search for Danice himself. Nor could Damien find out where the men who had snatched his sister had come from.

He tried not to think about it, and turned his attention back to the feast. At least it showed he could still provide for his family.

'I'm not sure how you eat this,' Damien said, holding a knife over the pineapple, a fruit he had seen once but never tasted.

'I'll show you,' Hanna said, getting up. Her crippled legs wobbled as the tree house swayed slightly in the wind.

Alli dashed to her side to support her.

'I'm all right!' Hanna pushed her away. 'Wind's a-rising, things will buckle and fold for a while. Don't bother me.'

Damien hated seeing his mother in this surly mood, especially as there was nothing he could say to make her feel better. Talking wouldn't bring Danice back.

He turned to the open window. Great banks of storm clouds brewed along the horizon and a rising wind ruffled the treetops. Lights flickered from the candles in the other tree houses. These days, they were inhabited mainly by women, young children and the elderly. Most of the adult men were gone, working as slaves, or as poorly paid factory workers in Old City.

'I better go and see Bigdad,' Damien said. 'I can give him a share of the food. And these . . .' He took a pair of scuffed leather boots from a hessian sack and showed them off proudly.

'Where did you get those?' Hanna asked. 'You didn't do some silly piece of trade, did you?'

'The Chieftain gave them to me,' Damien replied. 'I think they were going to be thrown out.'

His mother grunted. 'Trouble. Working for the Chieftain is causing us nothing but trouble.'

'A lot of the other families here are starving, Mama,' Damien reminded her. 'You know that. Working for the Chieftain is risky, but it puts food in our bellies!'

'Not unless we eat, it doesn't!' Hanna snapped. She reached for the pineapple. 'Cut the leaves off the top, trim the thick skin all around till you reach the flesh. Then eat it . . . if you have the appetite for it.'

Damien opened his bag and packed some of the chicken, a couple of apples, a few vegetables and the boots into it. 'I'll eat when I get back later tonight,' he said. He slung the bag over his shoulder. 'I'd better go while it's still light.'

'Be careful, Damien,' Alli said.

'Those people have already taken Danice,' Hanna added. 'How do you know you won't be next?'

'I'll be all right, Mama. I can look after myself,' Damien replied.

'Then watch out for the——' Hanna began, but Damien didn't wait to hear her out.

He stepped onto the timber landing outside. The wind in the soughing redwoods smothered his mother's voice. Damien didn't need reminding. He knew the dangers of the night.

'Care for what's left?' the Chieftain asked, taking the last portion of grilled steak from a platter on the table.

'No, boss, thank you,' O'Bray replied politely, and sat back a little in his chair.

'You prefer the synthetic stuff from the Farms?'

'Syn-food is nutritious, it's filling,' O'Bray said, 'and they say it's non-carcinogenic.'

'*This* is *real* food,' the Chieftain said, cutting into the meat and lifting a juicy chunk to his mouth.

O'Bray let his master eat. If that was the sort

of thing he liked, who was O'Bray to object? The Chieftain had different tastes and habits, acquired in the Far Lands. Or so he had said on the few occasions he had mentioned his origins.

O'Bray didn't enquire too deeply. Warlords like the Chieftain came and went all the time. This one had first arrived over a year ago, along with a great deal of gold. Enough to buy a large share of whatever technology was available in this unsophisticated world. And also enough gold to buy friendship with the Tribunes who lived a few kilometres away in Old City.

Gold meant power, and O'Bray knew this better than most. He worked for whoever paid the best price. For now, that person was the Chieftain.

'Mmm, delicious.' The Chieftain wiped his lips with a white napkin. 'Now, O'Bray, let's talk business.'

O'Bray bowed his head slightly. 'You wish to launch another gold-seeking operation?'

'A big one,' the Chieftain said. 'Winter's coming, and power from the nuclear station will cost us more. Also, the Tribunes are fond of their large and regular payments from my treasury. We need to get hold of as much gold as we can to last through the colder months, and into next year. What have you discovered?'

O'Bray had access to the library archives in Old City—access that cost them plenty of gold. 'There are two major prospects,' he said after a moment. 'The

United States Federal Gold Reserve in the twenty-first century. And there's a shipwrecked Portuguese treasure ship in the sixteenth century.'

'The Gold Reserve—what are our chances there?' the Chieftain asked.

'The gold there is worth a fortune, boss,' O'Bray replied, 'but from what I can discover, it's kept in very strong vaults with extremely high security.'

'Could we send a timeline into the building?'

'It's possible, but we would need reconnaissance,' O'Bray said. 'We'd need to check out the whole set-up first.'

The Chieftain frowned. 'Risky. And I don't want to lose another kid. Good ones are hard enough to find and train as it is.' He thought a moment. 'And the ship?'

'It was wrecked off the coast of Sumatra in 1515,' O'Bray said, 'carrying looted treasure from Malacca. Gold bars, coins, statuettes. A couple of tonnes at least, is my estimate.'

'The exact location?' the Chieftain asked.

'Washed up on a beach. There is a tiny fishing village a kilometre or two along the coast, but no other inhabitants.'

'An easy in-and-out for our team, then?'

'Yes,' O'Bray agreed. 'If we pick the right time—and the right weather.'

'I'll think about it,' the Chieftain said. 'Meanwhile, you can do something else for me.'

'Of course, boss, anything.'

The Chieftain picked up his knife and fork. 'Pass that mustard, will you? Steak's nothing without the bite of extra-hot mustard.'

The tunnel reeked of sewage and chemical waste. Damien crept along a narrow path at the side of a thick stream of stinking swill that flowed out of the city. He was breathing hard and sweating and was glad to be nearing the end. With only fifty metres to go, he could see the steel grid at the tunnel mouth ahead and a glimpse of light beyond.

Damien reached the grid and took a gulp of fresh air. The well-worn nuts and bolts keeping the grid in place had been loosened many times. It took only a minute to remove them and to swing the grid inward on its hinges.

He crept cautiously out of the tunnel and crawled up a narrow embankment. The ten-metre-high stone wall that surrounded the city was now immediately behind him. The sewerage tunnel was the only way of getting into the city from the forest without being checked by guards. It was a route that no one but the poor and the desperate could bring themselves to use.

Damien crouched and waited for a few seconds at the top of the embankment. There was an open space between the wall and the first houses, and guards regularly patrolled the wall. Damien had to be watchful. To be caught here, and to give away the secret uses of the tunnel, would be a disaster. Without the tunnel, Damien would most likely never see his father again.

The way was clear, so Damien dashed across the open space and into a dirty alley between a row of unpainted wooden houses. He stopped at one of the doors, glanced up and down the street and knocked four times.

'Trip you up!' said a man's voice.

'Only if you catch me,' Damien murmured. These were lines from a game he had once played with his sisters.

The door opened and a bear-like man appeared in the frame. 'Out of the street—quick!' he said.

Damien slipped inside and the door closed silently behind him. The welcoming hand of his father gripped his shoulder. 'Damien, good to see you! How's the family?'

'They're all right, Bigdad.'

'And further news about Danice?' Lines of worry made his face look even older than usual. The word had been brought to Bigdad earlier in the day.

'Nothing. We still don't know who took her,' Damien said, and hurried through the details of the incident. 'Then I just ran off,' he finished. 'I went back to the timeline and left.' He hung his head. 'I don't know how to forgive myself.'

Bigdad put an arm around his son's shoulders. 'You reacted quickly, as best you could in the circumstances. There was nothing else you could have done.'

'That's what I keep telling myself,' Damien replied unhappily. He unhitched his bag. 'Anyway, I brought you food—plenty of it. And a pair of boots as well.'

'Thanks. Now, sit down, son. In a while we'll talk some more.'

Damien slumped onto the old couch, letting his head fall back on the cushion. Sometimes the pressure was too hard to bear—the food-carrying trips; skulking through the dark streets at night; the endless, wearying trips through time. And now Danice's disappearance.

Perhaps for the next few hours he could pretend it didn't matter. He could just enjoy the warmth of his father's company before returning to the tunnel and the perils of the world beyond.

14

'Come on fella—*hup! Hup!'*

Simon urged the grey gelding into the woods at the northern boundary of Mayfield Manor's grounds. Low branches whipped past his head as the horse extended his stride into a canter. Simon had ridden as often as possible since that first lesson, and his confidence had grown. He liked it like this, with the wind full and fresh in his face and the hoofs of his horse pounding the turf. Maxi seemed to enjoy being pushed to the limit. Weaving through the trees, they raced back out into the open.

'Good boy!' Simon yelled. He gave Maxi his head and they shot towards the hedge at the bottom of the field. 'One more round of the course, old fella, then we'll call it a day.'

Just then the alarm pinged on his wristwatch. Maxi nickered.

'Easy, easy now!' Simon said, checking the time.

'Geez—I forgot! I'm late for training!'

Simon enjoyed the way that riding helped him forget his worries, but this time he had taken it too far. If he missed training, he might be banned from his missions.

Simon turned Maxi and spurred him into a gallop. Even so, it took him five minutes to get back to the stables.

'Maeve! Hey, Maeve!' Simon called, sliding out of the saddle.

The young woman mucking out the yard looked up at him wearily. 'In a hurry, then?' she asked.

'Sorry. Really sorry. I'm late for training. Can you unsaddle Maxi and give him a rub-down? Please, big favour!'

'Sure, but you owe me one. *Another one!*'

'I won't forget!' Simon called, sprinting out of the stable yard. He still had to get up to the manor house and change before getting off to training.

At the main training field, Simon sneaked to the back of the line of temponauts. It had taken him five minutes to change into his full training suit (a simulated version of his real time-travel suit) and then run to the field. He was twenty minutes late.

'So, you made it!' Nick said, turning around with a grin.

'Savage! Front and centre!' Cutler ordered.

Simon grimaced, then sauntered past the others and stepped out in front. He came rigidly to attention.

Cutler glared at him. 'So, you've decided to join us!'

'Yes, sir!'

'Twenty minutes late means twenty laps round the jogging track—when we've finished,' Cutler said. 'Is that clear?'

Don't debate, Simon told himself, you're in enough trouble. 'Sir! Yes, sir!' he said.

'Back in line!' Cutler barked. 'And Spenser . . .?'

'Sir!'

'Next time you speak out of turn, you do twenty laps as well. Understood?'

'Sir! Yes, sir!'

'All right,' Cutler said. 'Savage, we've already warmed up in your absence. You'll have to catch up as best you can.'

'Yes, sir!' Simon replied.

'We'll continue basic training,' the captain continued, addressing the group as a whole. 'In particular, with the springers in your shoes.'

The temponauts glanced nervously at the obstacle course awaiting them. There were five walls built from logs, and at heights of one, three, five, seven and nine metres. There was a five-metre gap between each wall.

'I've seen from your mission reports that a few of you have already tested the camouflage aspects of your travel suits.' Cutler's eyes flicked towards Simon, Danice and Ivan. 'And that you have done so under field conditions.

'But I'm not satisfied you're showing the same skills with your springers. Yesterday, we tackled the one-metre and three-metre walls. Most of you did all right.'

Nick stared down at the ground.

'Well might you look at your miserable feet, Spenser,' Cutler said. 'This isn't the football field, you know. You're not kicking a ball. Learn to use your feet in other ways. More discipline—more coordination!'

Nick nodded sheepishly.

'You were all chosen for this job because you already have strong athletic abilities,' Cutler went on. 'Surfing, survival skills, football, track and field, swimming. So, use those skills, and train hard. And for heaven's sake learn to use your springers properly. They can get you out of difficult situations. They can save your life! Understood?'

'Sir! Yes, sir!' the temponauts chorused.

Cutler walked along the line, eyeing each temponaut in turn. 'Now, a few points to remember about the operation of your springers. First, activate your springers with your wrist pilot. And remember, activation works for only one jump. You must reactivate your springers each time you jump.'

'Yes, sir!' the temponauts replied.

'But there may be situations where you might need to make one, two or more jumps in sequence.' Cutler glanced out into the field. 'Like today's obstacle course. What do you do under these circumstances—eh, Savage?'

'After you finish the first jump, you pause,' Simon replied. 'You rock back on your heels and the springers automatically reactivate. Sir!'

'Good. You've learnt something, at least,' Cutler said. 'Very well, Simon and Danice, you're first. Take your positions.' He turned to the other temponauts. 'You have permission to encourage them!'

Simon and Danice jogged to the start—a white line painted five metres from the first wall.

'Engage your springers!' Cutler ordered.

Simon and Danice activated the command *SPRING SHOES* on their wrist pilots and with a click the soles of their springers rose another four centimetres.

'Remember to adopt your landing position when you come out of the jumps,' Cutler said. 'Ready? Go!'

Together, Simon and Danice stepped back and then sprang forward, feet together. They hit the ground at the same time and bounced into the air, leaping easily over the one-metre wall.

'A cinch!' Simon said.

'Try and catch me!' Danice quickly rocked back and leapt forward again.

Simon rushed his move on the second jump and

hit the ground off-balance. He lurched at an angle across the three-metre wall but just managed to land in the correct crouching position.

'She got ya, surfie boy!' Nick called out.

'Good one, Danice!' Taylor joined in.

Simon barely heard them. Despite the fumble, he quickly recovered his balance. He focused on the wall ahead. He rocked back, jumped hard and bounced cleanly, clearing the five-metre barrier a fraction behind Danice.

She flashed him a smile of triumph as they simultaneously leapt over the next wall.

'You're at nine metres!' Cutler yelled. 'Don't forget to somersault the higher jump!'

Together, Simon and Danice rocketed into the air and into their somersaults. But Danice faltered as she came out of the turn, bumping her shoulder on the top of the wall and careering against Simon. They dropped like stones onto the thick padded matting at the base of the wall.

Simon groaned. His arms, legs and chest throbbed with pain. He took a tentative deep breath, then pushed himself up from the mat. There was no major damage.

He glanced at Danice. She lay motionless.

'Danice!' He crawled over and touched her shoulder. 'Danice!'

For a second, she didn't move. Then her eyes flickered open and she sucked in a deep breath.

'You all right? You injured?' Simon asked.

'Wind . . . ed,' Danice croaked. 'Sorry . . . all that . . . my fault.'

'Savage! Report!' Cutler bellowed from the far side of the walls. 'Are you two all right?'

'Sir! Yes, sir!' Simon yelled back.

'Your day's not over, Savage,' Cutler shouted. 'The jogging track—now!'

Simon nodded to Danice. 'Take it easy.' Then he called back to the captain. 'Sir! Yes, sir!'

And he jogged off to complete his punishment.

15

'This is planet Earth in the twenty-fourth century,' the tall woman with frizzy red hair announced from the front of the main classroom. Her name was Sandra Creele, and she was the Bureau's Head of Mission Mapping.

Professor McPhee turned in his seat to Simon and Danice. 'I've invited only you two because this is a special briefing. The year 2321 is your next mission.'

'It would pay to give this your full attention,' Captain Cutler added from the back of the room.

Simon was tense with excitement. Here was a chance to see what the Time Bureau was really up to. He glanced at Danice. 'Hey, we'll be the first temponauts into the future,' he whispered.

'I'll just be going home,' Danice replied.

Simon nodded. 'Yeah, suppose you're right.'

They looked up at the image of Earth projected on the widescreen television behind Sandra Creele. The image rotated from Europe to the Mediterranean, then to India, Asia, Australia and the Pacific Ocean.

'Hey, what happened to all the land?' Simon exclaimed. 'Big chunks of land are missing from the continents. And the oceans look much wider!'

'Don't ask me,' Danice said. 'We don't have maps of the world where I come from.'

'As Simon has so succinctly pointed out,' Creele said, 'the world changes significantly in the three hundred years between now and the twenty-fourth century. Ten thousand years of fairly stable climate will have come to an end. A major part of this will have been caused by global warming.'

She punched a key on a notebook PC and the picture froze on a satellite view of Europe. 'By the year 2100, the Arctic sea ice has completely gone and the Greenland Ice Sheet has almost disappeared. This alone will raise sea levels around the world by about seven metres. Glaciers melting in northern Europe, South America and other countries will push up ocean levels even further, meaning countries like the Netherlands will be almost entirely underwater.'

Simon leaned forward, taking in every word.

'Here, in the countries around the Mediterranean and in Africa, there are massive water shortages between the twenty-first and twenty-fourth centuries, and there is a state of almost permanent drought,' Creele said, indicating the relevant areas with a red laser pointer. 'Agriculture has rapidly declined, along with a massive fall in the population.'

Creele punched another key and the image rotated to Asia and Australia.

'You'll also see that the landmass of Bangladesh is gone,' she said. 'Along with other parts of coastal India, China and South-East Asia. In fact, twenty million hectares of mangrove forests have disappeared from tropical and sub-tropical zones around the world. These were areas that used to provide food, fuel and building materials for about six hundred million people. All these populations have disappeared.

'In Australia,' Creele went on, 'the huge Kakadu area in the Northern Territory is now covered by sea water, and the Great Barrier Reef in Queensland has been killed off. Most of the original coastline is also underwater.'

'Isn't that where you live?' Danice whispered. 'On the coast?'

Simon nodded. For a moment, he wondered what would happen to his own home. Would Bondi simply disappear under the sea? It didn't bear thinking about.

'And if we direct our attention to the Pacific Ocean, most of the islands are not there any more,' Creele said.

'What about the place you call America, ma'am?' Danice asked.

'I'll get to that in a minute,' Creele said, turning to

the screen. 'The world of the twenty-fourth century is one of contrasts. There are huge areas of desert on some continents, huge areas of steamy swamps on others. In fact, it is similar to the Cretaceous swamps during the last age of the dinosaurs. There are also similar levels of carbon dioxide in the atmosphere as there were then.

'This has had a catastrophic effect on food crops, and as a result, Earth's population in 2321 is maybe two billion people, probably fewer. That's less than one-third of today's population.'

'Two out of three people have died,' Danice murmured.

'Is this because of food shortages, ma'am?' Simon asked. 'Because of the climate changing and the storms—things like that? How could so many people just . . . die?'

'All of those factors played a part,' Creele replied. 'But this has not all happened at once. Over a three hundred year period, populations have perished through other causes, too. Wars have been fought over water resources, and there have been huge plagues of malaria and dengue fever.'

Creele swung the red pointer towards the United States. 'Danice, you asked about America. Big earthquakes hit California in the late twenty-first century. You can see that a section of the pre-earthquake coastline has now disappeared. There is no Los Angeles, no San Francisco.'

'*Phew!*' Simon said. 'So are there any cities left?'

'There are pockets of advanced civilisation in Europe, South Africa, India, China, Japan, Australia and the eastern USA. But cities like ours today are gone,' Creele said. 'In most countries, there are isolated populations living in conditions similar to the few hunter–gatherer societies left here in the twenty-first century. Some oil-based fuel is still used, but the age of oil is mostly over. Wind, solar and nuclear power is used extensively. International travel is rare. Those who travel go by airship and boat, not by plane.'

Simon and Danice sat in stunned silence. Simon, because he couldn't believe what was going to happen. Danice, because she couldn't believe what had already happened.

'Over the past few months, we have sent hundreds of Time Positioning Satellites to view the Earth and map it every year between now and 2321.' Creele glanced at McPhee, who nodded, and then at Simon. 'You already know that we have discovered a time-travel system operating somewhere in 2321.'

Simon nodded, 'I saw the timelines on the Operations Screen.'

Creele hit another key and brought up a high-altitude aerial picture of a massive forest. She turned to Danice. 'I think this is what you call Big Forest.'

'That's where we live,' Danice confirmed. 'But it's never looked like that to me.'

'These pictures were taken a few days ago, in Danice's time, in the year 2321,' Creele said. 'The redwood forests have expanded greatly in three hundred years. Due to a warm, wet and foggy climate, they now cover large areas of what we call northern California, Oregon and Washington State.'

'If this is a photo of my home, does this mean you've been spying on us?'

'They do that a lot,' Simon whispered.

Cutler cleared his throat behind them. 'Only since we became aware that time travellers were being sent from this timezone,' he said. 'Travellers like you, Danice.'

Danice nodded. 'The Chieftain sends us.'

'There are now all sorts of wild animals living in this forest,' Creele said. 'Feral boars, dogs, lions, tigers, even elephants.'

'What—in North America?' Simon turned to Danice. 'Is this true?'

'You bet.'

'This is a different North America,' McPhee said, scratching his beard with his long fingers. 'The ancestors of these creatures probably escaped from zoos during the water wars, then bred and spread into the forests.'

'That's why we live high in the trees,' Danice added.

Creele changed the screen to a close-up image. It showed a section of the forest, as well as a rocky escarpment and what looked like a walled city. Three large buildings in the centre were surrounded by roads, laneways and thousands of smaller structures.

'That's what you call Old City,' Cutler said to Danice. 'Naturally, you've never seen it from this angle, but if you look closely, you might recognise some landmarks.'

Danice stood up and stepped closer to the screen. She pointed at the larger buildings. 'These towers are where the Tribunes live.'

'Who are they, exactly?' McPhee asked. 'We know very little of the political situation.'

'They're our . . . rulers,' Danice replied. 'Not very nice people. But we have to do what they say.'

'What do you mean?' McPhee asked. 'Do they use force? Fear?'

Danice bit her lips, nervous about being the centre of attention. She glanced from the screen, to McPhee, to Cutler and back to the screen again.

'There are only three Tribunes,' she explained. 'But they have soldiers and guards. If you ignore their orders, or refuse to work for them, or pinch food from the stores, then they send you to the Prison Farms. Or make you a slave in the factories.' She took a shaky breath. 'They took my father and made him a slave because he was trying to help people escape from the city. And he was trying to set up a school.'

'A school in the forest?' Simon asked.

Danice nodded. 'Though people get punished for a lot less than that. My dad was a teacher for a while, that's why I can read and write. A bit, anyway. The Tribunes have special teachers for their own kids, and for the kids of their friends. But, mostly, no one can read or write.'

'Tell us about this Chieftain that you mentioned,' McPhee said.

'We work for him.' Danice pointed to the screen. 'His fortress is just there, south of the city.'

Creele hit a key and the screen changed to an image of a walled compound on the cliff edge, with a few stone buildings and a couple of visible cave entrances.

'That looks like it,' Danice said. 'You see? Those two big gates are in the wall around the caves where he lives.' She moved even closer to the screen. 'The gate in the north wall is for the road to the city, and the one on the western wall is where we come and go from the forest.'

'Are you saying this Chieftain lives in a cave?' Simon asked.

'Yeah, the cave entrance is there.' Danice pointed to a dark patch on the escarpment, about a hundred metres from the northern gate. 'But it's well set up inside. A room with a big throne, lots of furniture. Kind of . . .'

'Luxurious,' McPhee suggested.

'Yes,' Danice replied. 'He gives us special

food. Not Syn-food, but real food, fresh meat and vegetables. He's not short of anything.'

'Do you go on your time-trips from these caves?' Simon asked.

'Yeah, but from deep underground,' Danice replied. 'There's this big tunnel and a Time Accelerator, just like the one here.'

'So now we're narrowing things down!' exclaimed McPhee. 'Perhaps we could have the next picture, Sandra?'

'Right. Further inland, on the eastern side of Old City, there's this structure,' Creele said, showing an image of a big square building with a colossal domed structure to one side. 'It's a nuclear power station, a few kilometres from the centre of the city, but still within the city walls. It's over a hundred years old. However, it's been rebuilt several times and it's well maintained.'

'I've seen it from a distance,' Danice said. 'But no one I know has ever been in there.'

'We believe it might provide the power for this Chieftain's time-travel missions,' Cutler said.

McPhee stood up and joined Danice by the screen. He put a hand on her shoulder. 'Thank you for explaining these things to us,' he said. 'This is the reason we brought you here. I apologise for the way it happened, but if we had made ourselves known to you, instead of taking you by surprise, your brother would have pushed you into your own timeline and we would have lost you.' He paused. 'And we need you because of your intimate knowledge of your home.'

That's why the Time Bureau needs Danice, Simon thought. But what's in it for her? She seemed to have taken her kidnapping amazingly well. But maybe she had no choice. Simon knew from his experience that the Bureau were good at getting people to do what they wanted.

'So, sir, why do you need me?' he asked. 'I don't know anything about Danice's time at all.'

'All you need to know is that your role is important,' McPhee replied.

'You're the two fittest and the best qualified for the job,' Cutler explained. 'Danice, because of your knowledge, and Simon because of your energy and your nerve. You'll need each other.'

Simon and Danice exchanged a quick glance.

'Your mission has three objectives,' Cutler continued. 'The first is to enter Old City, and to observe the current situation there. We want you to see how much control the Tribunes and their forces have over the local people.'

Simon nodded.

'We want you to do this quickly while on the way to checking out the power station. Your second objective is to assess the security there, then attempt to enter the facility and find out if it's definitely the source of the power for this Chieftain's time-travel system.'

'It's important that we have this basic information,' McPhee added.

'Your third and most important objective is to learn more about this Chieftain,' Cutler said. 'Such as, who he is, exactly, where he keeps his Time Accelerator, and what are his immediate plans. And any other information you can find.'

'We're giving you forty-eight hours,' McPhee added. 'Understood?'

'Yes, sir!' they both replied.

Simon frowned. 'I have one question about this Chieftain guy. Do we know why he's using time travel?'

'Danice?' McPhee lifted a questioning eyebrow. 'Would you like to tell him?'

'The Chieftain's after gold,' Danice said.

'But we don't know why,' McPhee added. 'It seems easier for him to steal it from the treasure houses of history than to mine it for himself.'

'Maybe there's no gold left in the ground in the twenty-fourth century,' Simon said.

'Whatever the reason, it is something we're planning to stop,' McPhee said. 'We can't allow future citizens to steal the world's reserves of gold. It could wreck the economies of both past and present nations.' He paused and gazed almost kindly at Simon and Danice. 'So, are you ready for this mission?'

'It would be a good idea to read your brief thoroughly, Savage,' Cutler said. 'This is Danice's home, but for you it is the future. It is a very different world.'

'I'll be ready, don't worry, sir,' Simon replied.

His nerves tingled, though he couldn't tell if it was excitement or terror. He would be the first temponaut to travel into the future. But it was dangerous. A leap into the unknown. Would he survive the experience? If he didn't, there would be no one left to find out the truth behind his father's death.

'Hi, Harry,' Simon said an hour later, and sat down at the command console in front of the Timeline Operations Screen. 'I'm here for my Time Control and Mission Tracking System session.'

'You're on a mission first thing tomorrow,' Harry replied. 'We can do this when you get back, if you like.'

'It's okay, I'm too nervous to relax.' Simon looked up at the range of clocks across the timezones and ages. It was after nine o'clock Present Time but he didn't want to miss any opportunity of seeing how Time Control worked. 'Is it all go for tomorrow?'

Harry toggled a few keys and a blue Future Mission Line appeared to the year 2321.

'All systems are ready. The Spin Box is already charging up and your TPS is on standby.' He grinned at Simon. 'The future, eh? S'pose you know you're making history.'

'So they reckon,' Simon said. 'But Danice is going

to the future, too, except she's kind of going back there.'

'Still, they'll probably put up your picture in the entrance foyer one day.'

Simon laughed. 'Oh, sure. So who can look at it? No one ever comes to Mayfield and no one knows what we do.'

'Yep, it's tough. We don't get rich, we don't get famous and we still have to work the late shift.' Harry grinned. 'So, what shall we do tonight?'

I've been thinking about this for weeks, Simon thought. I want to work out how to get back to where Dad disappeared. Only I don't want to let Harry know that's what I'm doing.

'I'll be getting plenty of the future tomorrow,' Simon said. 'So how about you show me how to send a TPS somewhere in the past?'

'Sure, why not? We've got another satellite on standby, we can play around with that one,' Harry said. 'You know the protocols for establishing a timeline?'

Simon tried to recall the exact procedure. 'Um, access code, handprint, get clearance . . .'

'Okay, take it one at a time. Put in your code.'

Simon punched his six-number security code onto the keypad. The words: *ACTIVATE PRINT CLEARANCE* appeared.

'All in the fingers, mate,' Harry said. 'We conquer time with our fingers. But don't rush it.'

Simon carefully placed his right hand on a flat glass touchplate.

'*You—have—clearance!*' came the electronic reply.

'I hate that voice,' Simon said.

'They say it's the prof's voice specially re-recorded, just to freak us out.' Harry smiled. 'Is there any particular past date you have in mind?'

Simon thought carefully. After being recruited by the Bureau, he had memorised the geographic coordinates of the beach where his father's car had been found. He had also memorised the approximate time of his disappearance. 'Um, Kiama Beach, south of Sydney, November ninth last year,' he said coolly. 'About three p.m.'

Harry chuckled. 'Got dumped by a big wave there, eh?'

'Yeah, sort of.'

'Okay, let's put the TPS on standby,' Harry said. He typed in the coordinates and a series of commands from a manual that lay open by his right hand. 'Then I hit *ACTIVATE*. Got it?'

Simon nodded and kept his eyes on the Timeline Operations Screen. A second later, a red flag flashed at the start of the timeline.

Harry raised his eyebrows. 'Huh? That's unusual. It's red-flagged.'

'Why? What's that mean?'

'For some reason, normal access to that time and

that location is off-limits. It happens. Sometimes they bar particular timezones. Is it significant?'

Simon quickly checked out Harry's body language. Did he know more than he was saying? But one look at Harry's open manner made Simon relax.

'No, I just made it up on the spot,' Simon lied.

'Well, no worries then.'

Simon took a long look at the red flag. No access. Why would the Bureau stop a TPS going back to that day? Were they hiding something?

Simon pretended to yawn. Now all he wanted to do was get back to his room—and think about what that timezone bar might mean. 'Hey, you know, I might call it a night after all.'

'We've only done ten minutes. Do you want to end the lesson?'

'Yeah, reckon I will. I am feeling a bit tired.'

'All right,' Harry replied. 'We can take this up again when you return.'

'Okay, Harry, thanks,' Simon said, heading for the exit.

'Good luck on the mission!' Harry called out, watching him go. Then he frowned, reached for his clipboard and jotted a few notes on the evening report sheet.

Simon shuffled into the garden and looked beyond the cloudy sky to the distant stars. Tonight, the stars seemed even further away than ever.

16

The 24th Century, North America

Simon opened his eyes, blinked a few times and felt a brief surge of dizziness. Then he scrambled to his feet, found his balance and spotted Danice nearby. 'Hi—are you all right?' he said.

'Yeah, I feel a bit woozy, but I'm here.'

'So we made it.' They were standing on a roughly made wooden platform high in the treetops. Simon touched his wrist pilot to retract his helmet. The musty smell of wet trees filled his nostrils and the timbers under his feet creaked as the trees swayed in the cool pre-dawn wind.

First things first, he thought, switching off the Zone Activator on his wrist pilot. The hovering TPS vanished and the wormhole dissolved.

'Better check our location, too,' Simon said.

'I know where we are. This is the right place,' Danice said, retracting her own helmet. 'Follow me—this way!'

She stepped onto a rope-and-plank suspension bridge that connected their platform to another tree platform about forty metres away.

Simon followed.

'You can't tell in this light, but we're about sixty metres up,' Danice said. 'Just stay along the middle of the bridge and walk steadily. If you don't move too much from side to side it won't rock. And don't look down if it makes you feel weird.'

'I don't mind the height,' Simon replied. 'That isn't what's making me feel weird right now. Where are we going?'

'To my house!'

'Right, I knew that.'

Simon soon found a steady pace as they walked from bridge to bridge through the dense forest canopy. The bridges were like an elevated trail above the ground—a series of suspended walkways linked together so the tree-dwellers could move from one section of the forest to another without having to risk their lives on the forest floor.

As they walked, the sun rose and the sky lightened. All around, the spires of thousands of massive trees spread far into the misty distance.

'Awesome!' Simon breathed. He still couldn't believe he was really in the twenty-fourth century.

'Take a look down there.' Danice pointed to the ground below.

A striped feline body flashed across the forest floor.

'What's that?' Simon asked.

'A tiger, I think.'

'A tiger?'

'Yeah, there's a few in this part of the forest,' Danice replied.

Suddenly there was a swishing sound and an arrow thumped into the trunk in front of Simon.

'*Sheesh*—watch out!' he cried, jumping back.

Danice tore the arrow from the bark and checked the three feathered vanes at the notched end. Clearly, she recognised them because she laughed.

'This is funny—someone shooting at us?' Simon asked. 'Is that what you do for kicks around here?'

Danice ignored him and looked across to another colossal tree, a hundred metres away across a gully. 'Alli!' she yelled. 'Alli!'

Simon saw that a dwelling had been built ingeniously in the tree's topmost branches. On the platform outside there was a girl. She started jumping up and down and waving her arms.

'Danice! Danice!' she screamed. Her cries echoed through the forest.

'Someone's glad to see you,' Simon said.

'It's my sister,' Danice said with a grin. 'A few more bridges and we'll be there. Just follow me.'

'They've been successfully inserted,' Harry reported. 'They're in the neutral zone now, sir. The TPS has withdrawn. Shall I program the satellite to return to the same location in forty-eight hours?'

Cutler nodded. 'Yes, that's the mission schedule.'

Harry looked at the timeline and grimaced. 'We could have delivered them closer to Old City.'

'Not worth the risk,' Cutler replied. 'The Chieftain would be more likely to pick up their timeline if we opened it too near his cave.'

'That's if he's got the sort of equipment that will detect these things, sir.'

'Well, there are things we know about him, and there are things we don't know,' the captain said. 'It's up to Simon and Danice to find out what it is we don't know.'

In the tree house, Simon was surrounded by Danice's family.

'And what did you do to Danice?' Damien asked. 'Where did she go? Where's she been all this time?'

'Damien, ease off!' Danice said. 'I just got back. I'm safe! I'm here! Stop asking all these stupid questions.'

Damien scowled at Simon's suit. 'And that gear you're wearing. You're dressed like those guys who took Danice in the first place. Where are you from? What are you up to?'

'I'm just doing my job,' Simon said. 'I was told to bring Danice back, and that's what I've done.' It was a pretty lame explanation, Simon thought, but that was his official excuse. He would have to stick with it.

Damien shot an accusing glance at Danice. 'What have they got you involved in?'

'They don't mean us any harm,' Danice said. 'Believe me, they're better organised than the Chieftain and they've promised to help us.'

'Help, how? And who are *they*?' Damien said.

This was also news to Simon. 'No one told me about any help,' he said.

'Sorry, Simon,' Danice replied. 'I wasn't allowed to say until I got here. I had my own special briefing, you see.' She glanced at Hanna and Alli. 'They promised me that if I helped them, then they'd try to get Bigdad out of Old City and get us all back together again. Even relocate us. Somewhere safer.'

'That explains a lot,' Simon said. 'I wondered why you were so helpful after being as good as kidnapped by the Bureau. Is this why you agreed to become a temponaut for them?'

Danice smiled with a brief shrug of her shoulders.

'Your father?' Hanna's eyes lit up as she struggled up from her wooden chair. 'Back with us. And you, too, Danice!'

Simon stepped forward to give Hanna a hand.

'It's okay, let me do it,' Alli said, quickly taking Hanna's arm. 'Mama doesn't like people to fuss. A year ago, she broke both her legs. The planks of the walkways rot easily and sometimes they snap.'

'A lot of people fall,' Hanna said, shrugging it off. 'I'm not to be singled out for it.'

'I can help all of us,' Danice said to Damien. 'Maybe make our life a bit easier. Let Simon and me complete our mission.'

'What mission?' Damien glared at Simon again. 'A moment ago he said he was just here to see you home. Now you're talking about a mission! I don't trust him. I'm not letting you go——'

Suddenly there was the rapid thrum of drums in the distance.

Damien sprang to the open window and looked into the sky.

'What is it?' Hanna asked anxiously.

A series of blasts from a ram horn echoed through the forest.

'Four short—four long!' Damien turned back into the room. 'It's a raid! We have to get out!'

Simon looked at Danice. 'What do we do?'

'We've got two choices,' Danice said, pushing him towards the door. 'Get away—or get caught!'

17

The woodland, which an hour earlier had seemed quiet and empty, was now a riot of chaos and noise.

Three giant cigar-shaped airships hung in the sky. Scores of shouting, black-clad soldiers abseiled commando-style down ropes onto the walkways connecting the tree houses. In the surrounding groves, ram horns spread news of the raid. Hundreds of forest-dwellers poured down ladders and ropes to escape in a terrified stampede.

'Go!' Danice shouted down to Damien, as he helped his mother to the forest floor.

'We'll be at the Fire Caves!' Damien called back. He shepherded Hanna into the dim underbrush on the other side of the clearing.

Danice pointed to the east. 'We have to go that way—to the cliffs,' she said to Simon.

Suddenly a man screamed, *'Let me go, I've done nothing! Let me go!'*

Simon turned and spotted the man dangling from a rope tied tight around his ankles. He struggled helplessly as he was hauled into the cabin of the airship that hovered above.

'Hurry, or we'll end up like him!' Danice said, dragging Simon onto the next walkway.

'There—search that house!' a soldier's voice barked behind them.

Simon and Danice sprinted to the end of the walkway and flattened their bodies against the brown trunk of the next tree.

'I hope our camouflage kicks in quickly,' Simon whispered.

Two armed soldiers pounded past, burst into Hanna's house and started to trash the contents.

'They'll be busy for a while. Come on!' Danice said, darting onto another walkway.

Behind them, the forest resonated with sharp shouts as soldiers continued their sweep of the area.

'What's going on?' Simon asked, sprinting to keep up with Danice. 'Who are these guys?'

'They have black uniforms, which means they work for the Tribunes. They send out soldiers every month. They look for slaves who might have escaped from Old City,' Danice said.

'Isn't this part of the Chieftain's area?'

'Yeah, this is his part of the forest,' she replied, making a sharp turn around a tree and onto yet another swinging walkway. 'But the Tribunes don't care. They're more powerful than he is. They go where they like. And it isn't just slaves they're after. They round up anyone.'

Far behind them, the crying protests of another captive demonstrated her point.

Simon stopped mid-stride. 'So you're telling me the soldiers are taking them back to the city?'

Danice turned and gaped at him for a moment. Then she shook her head. 'No! I know what you're thinking.'

'Stop guessing and just listen,' Simon said, grabbing her arm. 'We can hitch a ride with them.'

'These guys are our enemies,' Danice hissed. 'They're ruthless.'

'Look, it's a simple situation. Either we spend ages crawling along that filthy tunnel you told me about, or we get to the city by airship, clean and fast!'

'You're crazy.'

Simon looked up at the nearest airship and the six ropes that dangled from it. 'I'm not saying we surrender to them,' he said. 'I'm saying we sneak on board and stow away.'

'What about the soldiers?'

Simon looked at the two airships furthest away from them. More captives were being hauled up by ropes into the open hatches of cabins which were attached under the hulls of the craft.

'They've got their hands full over there . . . but not here,' Simon said, carefully checking the cabin of the airship above. For the time being, it looked deserted. 'Look, we've probably got a few minutes before the soldiers start coming back with more captives.'

'And how do we get up there?'

Simon pointed to Danice's feet. 'Our springers. Wouldn't the captain call this "getting out of a difficult situation"?'

It took them only a minute to find their way to a spot directly below the ship.

'Up there?' Danice said doubtfully.

'Let's do it.' Simon punched the command *SPRING SHOES* on his wrist pilot and his shoes clicked into their 'ready' position. 'You reckon this platform's strong enough?' he asked. 'No rotting boards?'

Danice glanced down at the walkway and nodded. Then she stared up at the underbelly of the airship. 'But it must be fifty metres up to the hatch!'

'There's only a five-metre gap between us and the bottom of the ropes,' Simon pointed out. 'All right— are you ready?'

'Yep—we go together!'

'Okay.'

They ran forward two steps, hit the planks hard with their feet and sprang into the air. There was a moment of panic when they almost collided in midair. Then they grabbed the nearest ropes.

Simon spun around wildly as he tried to avoid crashing into Danice, who was twisting on her own rope.

'Get inside the ship, before they notice us!' Simon said, trying to steady himself. He hooked a loop of rope around his left shoe and started the upward climb. He glanced at Danice, who was struggling to bring her rope under control. 'You can climb, can't you?'

'I've been climbing trees since I was a baby!'

Together they shinnied swiftly up the ropes to the yawning black hatch of the airship's cabin.

'Any word on their progress?' Professor McPhee asked, glancing over Harry's shoulder at the Timeline Operations Screen.

'Not yet. Early days, sir.' Harry glanced at his superior. 'So to speak.'

McPhee went to stand beside Captain Cutler, who was quietly assessing the situation. 'This is the first time we've trusted a major mission to temponauts who aren't adults. What if they don't find out what we want to know?' he asked.

Cutler smiled. 'It's more a case of *who* they find, rather than what, isn't it?'

The professor nodded. 'You're right. We'll just have to wait and see what happens.'

The airship had been flying smoothly. But now it shook from end to end. Simon and Danice were hiding in the furthest corner of the passenger cabin.

They gripped a railing on the wall to stop themselves sprawling across the cabin floor.

'What's happening?' Danice whispered.

Simon lifted his head cautiously and peered over a pile of canvas tarpaulins and fuel barrels. A few metres away, four soldiers stepped amongst a group of about fifteen sullen forest-dwellers in leg chains.

'Come on, get up!' one soldier yelled, kicking a bearded man with the toe of his boot. 'Time to move!'

The man tried to lash out at his captor, but fell back as the ship lurched again.

Simon glanced at Danice. 'I think they're anchoring the ship.'

They stayed hidden as two soldiers unbolted and opened the main door.

'Move your lazy butts!' a soldier yelled, pushing the bearded man and a female prisoner through the opening and following them outside.

'Move! Move!' the other soldiers roared.

One by one, the rest of the prisoners shuffled through the door in their rattling chains. They were followed by their guards.

At last the cabin was empty.

Danice rose. 'Let's go——'

Simon suddenly dragged her back. 'Wait!' he hissed, as two uniformed pilots appeared from the front cockpit of the airship.

'We should get a bonus for capturing that hairy fellow again,' one man said.

'Bad luck for him—he escaped a couple of months ago,' the other replied. 'He'll go to the Prison Farms for sure this time.'

They stood for a moment at the door, looking at the string of prisoners being led down a set of steep metal stairs. Then they stepped out, laughing and chatting.

Simon and Danice waited a few moments more until they were sure the cabin was empty. Then they crept to the doorway and peered into the daylight.

The airship was floating high above the ground, moored by steel cables to a metal tower as high as a seven-storey building. Two similar towers formed a triangle in the airfield, with two other ships also secured at their berths. From that height, they could see a broad section of Old City and its chequerboard layout of buildings, streets and alleyways. Dotted around the edge of the city were as many as a dozen airships anchored to other towers.

'That looks like the only way out,' Simon said, pointing to where the crew, soldiers and prisoners were making their way down the stairs almost directly below them.

Danice grabbed Simon's arm. 'Hey, we've forgotten one thing.'

'What?'

'Clothes. Something to wear in the city over our suits,' she replied. 'I was supposed to get some clothes from Mama. But with the raid . . .'

'I saw something we might be able to use,' Simon said, heading back inside the cabin.

Danice brought up a map on her wrist pilot. 'I'll just check the exact location of the power station from here. It's about three-and-a-half kilometres that way—east.' She looked around. 'Hey, where are you?'

Simon came back with two pairs of worn, paint-spotted overalls and a couple of khaki caps. 'What about these?'

'Real attractive.' Danice smiled. 'But they'll do.'

Several minutes later, in disguise and having climbed down the tower, they sauntered into a crowded town square outside the airfield.

'What is this, some sort of carnival?' Simon asked.

'The open-air market,' Danice said. 'It's on every Saturday—the whole city turns out. For most people, it's the only time they get off work.'

Simon nodded and looked around the city square. A troupe of fire-breathing performers lit up a distant corner and a circle of eager children watched an elephant perform balancing tricks. Bumpy horse-drawn wagons trundled along a narrow, centre road, alongside new, shiny solar-powered cars. Neatly dressed shoppers haggled for bargains at pushcarts laden with bright clothes and knick-knacks, while ragged beggars called out for food or money.

Simon realised that the city square was a combi-nation of both the old and the new worlds. He also realised that he and Danice were two out of just a handful of people in all of history who had directly experienced both worlds for themselves.

But what Simon noticed most were the security guards and soldiers. They seemed to be everywhere: mean-looking men in blue or black uniforms, their eyes hidden behind wraparound sunglasses. All of them had thick leather belts bristling with batons, pistols, crowd-control sprays and handcuffs. Here was proof that the Tribunes and their men were in tight control of the city and its people, Simon thought. He could easily report that to the Time Bureau when they returned. He and Danice had achieved their first objective.

'Keep off the road! Keep off the road!' a guard roared at a cowering child.

'Don't stare,' Danice murmured to Simon. 'If you stare, he'll think you're challenging his authority. They don't like being challenged, believe me.'

Simon turned his head away and immediately tripped over a bag of spilt potatoes. He stumbled into the road. A horn blared. Danice grabbed him by the overalls and pulled him out of the path of an armoured minibus. 'Let's get out of here! You're attracting too much attention!'

She elbowed her way to the far side of the square with Simon in tow, then hauled him down a narrow lane and into the shadows.

As he was dragged along, Simon was glad Danice was leading the way. He felt out of his depth here in the future. But he knew he would have to get a grip on himself soon, if he wanted to make it back to the twenty-first century.

18

Rain lashed down through the dripping trees.

'How many of our people did they take?' Hanna asked. She was sitting on a log near the entrance of a giant, hollow redwood.

'Thirty, forty, no one's sure,' Damien replied, stepping inside and wiping the moisture from his face. 'Some might have escaped to the other hiding places.'

'Then we probably won't see them for a while,' Alli said. She huddled on a stool and pulled a possum-skin rug tight around her shoulders for warmth.

Damien swept dirt and leaves off a rickety wooden chair and sat down. A rush of tiredness swept over him. He badly needed to rest.

'Get yourself a drink,' Hanna said, pointing to the gourd of water on the makeshift table.

Damien gulped down a few mouthfuls and glanced around the inside of their temporary hide-out. It was many months since they had used the Fire Caves— soot-blackened chambers burnt deep into the boles of the trees by the wildfires that tore through the forests every decade or so. The hollow was the size of a small room, about three times Damien's height. It showed plenty of signs of non-human habitation. Spider webs hung from above in tangled strands, and the mossy floor was scattered with bird and animal droppings. On one side was a rough bed covered with more skins. There was also a dusty wooden shelf that held a few tins of Syn-food, a rusty hammer, a jar of bent nails, a bow, and a buckskin sheath of arrows. A metal-tipped spear leant against the wall.

'We'll probably have to hunt if we stay here much longer,' Alli said.

'There's plenty of game in this part of the forest,' Hanna agreed. 'There's deer and elk and possum.'

'Don't worry, I went back and fetched the bread and some of the fruit,' Damien said, tossing his bag on the bed. 'We can eat that. We won't have to hunt for a few days.'

He got up, walked to the entrance and looked out at the rain. 'I'm worried about Danice and that boy she's with.'

'Simon,' Alli said.

'Yeah, him.'

Damien didn't trust people he didn't know. Living hand-to-mouth and day-to-day, with the threat of slave raids and their precarious situation as the Chieftain's gold hunters, made him think like that. He only trusted the people he knew.

Damien was worried that Simon was in league with the people who had abducted Danice. Although Simon had brought his sister back, he was now leading her into dangerous situations without explaining why.

'Where's he from?' Damien asked. 'The past? The future? Who's he working for, and why won't he say why he's here?'

'Danice trusts him,' Alli replied, 'and she seems to know what she's doing.'

'Maybe she does. But whatever it is they're up to, I don't like it,' Damien said. 'I'm going to look for them.'

'Look for them?' Hanna protested. 'Where? You don't know what's happened to them or where they've gone!'

'Mama, you probably don't want to know this, but when I went back to get the food, someone told me they saw Danice and Simon climbing up into one of the airships.'

'That's stupid!' Alli cried. 'Why would they do that?'

Damien shrugged. 'To get into Old City, I suppose. That's what I have to find out.'

Hanna waved her hand irritably. 'Then go! Find her and bring her back. I want all my children here, with me. Safe.'

'Don't forget to block up the entrance,' Damien said, pointing to the sturdy wooden grate that his family would have to nail into place before dark. It was the only way to keep out the wildlings. 'Don't worry, Mama, I'll be all right.'

He stepped into the chilly afternoon and was gone.

'We're picking up a new timeline from 2321,' Harry reported to Captain Cutler.

'Is it anything to do with Simon and Danice's mission?' Cutler asked, leaning forward to examine the red line on the Operations Screen.

'This is totally new, sir. Sent by our mysterious Chieftain friend, I'd say.'

'An exploration satellite? Before they send out temponauts?'

'That's my calculation, sir.' Harry pointed to the other red timelines on the screen. 'In the past, they've sent one, two, or sometimes three TP Satellites to reconnoitre new locations.'

'Rather like we do,' Cutler said.

'We're usually more thorough than they are, sir.'

'To where does the timeline link?' Cutler asked.

'Indonesia, sir. 1515. The northern coast of Sumatra, to be exact. A fairly uninhabited area, by the looks of it.'

'Any intelligence on the area?'

'From around 1513, the Portuguese were very active in this region. They were after spices, sir, and . . .'

'Gold, yes, I know,' Cutler cut in. 'Do we have a TPS on standby?'

'Not at the moment,' Harry replied. 'But I can have one moving pretty soon.'

'Activate it, then. Investigate the location as soon as the satellite's operational.' Cutler frowned. 'What's that chieftain up to now?'

19

It was late afternoon. The yellow lights of the power station glinted dimly in the drizzle that fell from the darkening sky.

'Too many people at the front gate, there's no easy way in there,' Simon said, looking up from the clump of low bushes where he and Danice were hiding. He'd managed to calm himself down, and felt back in control.

'We'd better find some other way in,' Danice said. 'Our second objective is to find out if this is the source of the power for the Chieftain's time-travel system.'

Simon nodded.

He left their cover and crawled along a deep drainage ditch. Danice followed. Once they were out of sight of the gate they clambered up the bank and skirted along the base of the razor-wire fence that surrounded the station.

Danice looked up at the fence. 'It's about five metres high,' she said. 'Another job for our springers.'

'And the ground's pretty hard here,' Simon said, 'so let's fly.'

Retreating a few metres, they activated their wrist pilots and, on Simon's command, leapt forward, bouncing and soaring over the fence. They landed in the long grass on the other side.

Danice winced, lifting her right leg to reveal a jagged tear that had sliced through her suit to the flesh underneath. 'Ouch, that hurts!' she moaned. 'I snagged the top of that razor wire as we went over.'

Simon twisted around and took a small metal phial from his travel pouch. 'Try some of this repair solution,' he said. 'Stay still.'

The spray frothed over the wound. Within seconds, the cut in Danice's skin was healing. Tiny, dark threads appeared at the edges of the tear in her suit and began to reweave the fabric.

'How's that?' Simon asked.

'Better,' Danice said. 'I still can't figure out how that stuff works. But we should have kept it for an emergency.'

'It was an emergency!'

Danice managed a faint smile. 'I guess we don't make too bad a team, after all.'

Simon turned to the power station that loomed over them. 'So, let's find a way in.'

Danice pointed to a ramp and a set of double doors

at the side of the main building. One door was open, and two casually dressed workers were unloading cartons from the back of a truck and stacking them at the base of the ramp. 'Over there might be a good place to start,' she said.

'It looks like a loading bay,' Simon said. 'We can be part of their delivery.'

They crept silently through the long grass, keeping their heads down until they reached the edge of the parking bay.

'Wait,' Simon said. He watched as the men picked up a carton each, strolled lazily up the ramp and through the open door into the power station. He estimated that there was about thirty metres of open space between them and the ramp. 'We'll have to run,' he whispered.

'My leg's okay,' Danice replied. 'Just say when.'

'Now!'

They dashed across the parking area, up the ramp and disappeared inside the power station.

'I suppose you're wondering why I've asked you all here,' Professor McPhee said with a quick smile and a probing gaze at the small gathering in front of the Operations Screen. The three temponauts, Nick Spenser, Taylor Bly and Ivan Ho made up a tight group, while Captain Cutler stood beside Harry at the control desk.

'You're planning to send us on a big mission, sir,' Nick said glibly.

'Correct,' McPhee said, 'but I'll get to that soon.' He nodded to Harry. 'Activate the new locators.'

'Coming on now,' Harry replied, hitting a couple of keys. 'Look at the bottom-right of the screen, Professor.'

All eyes quickly fixed on a map of the west coast of the United States. Then the picture faded into a continuous stream of night vision from a darkened complex of buildings.

'The year is 2321,' the professor explained. 'This is where Simon and Danice are working right at this moment.'

'They're in the future!' Ivan gasped.

'I can't believe it—they never told us!' Nick said.

'What's that we're looking at?' Taylor asked.

'A power plant, some distance inland from the northern coast of California,' Harry said.

'We can see it with our new satellite,' Cutler added. 'We've put it into orbit around the Earth in the twenty-fourth century. Every ninety minutes it gives us the exact position of our temponauts, using micro-transmitters that we've embedded into your suits.'

'Is this something new?' Nick asked.

'Yes, we're trialling it on this mission.'

Nick grinned. 'Bet they don't know they're being tracked.'

'We weren't sure the system would work effectively,' Professor McPhee went on. 'It was best they didn't know, in case it failed when they were relying on it.'

'Seems to be functioning okay, sir,' Harry said.

'So, those two red dots flashing on the screen,' Ivan said, taking a closer look, 'they're Simon and Danice?'

McPhee nodded. 'And by the looks of it, they're right inside the power plant.'

'The dots aren't moving,' Taylor observed. 'Are they okay?'

'That's one thing the locators can't reveal exactly,' Cutler replied. 'They could be in trouble, or they could be simply taking in the view, or talking, or hiding. We don't know. The important thing is to keep monitoring them.'

'So, while they're running around in the twenty-fourth century, what do we do, Prof?' Nick asked.

'Now that you've seen what Simon and Danice are doing, we have a job for the three of you,' McPhee said. 'Sumatra, in the year 1515. Your job is to prevent one heck of a gold robbery.'

'We've been here twenty minutes. We can't wait all night,' Danice said, glancing at the security camera that was fixed just below the ceiling of a corridor deep inside the power station. 'You think they've seen us yet?'

'They would have been here long ago if they had,' Simon replied, checking the entry handprint-reader for the tenth time. He was trying to work out some way of overriding it, so they could get through the security doors and further inside. 'The electronic security's tight, but there don't seem to be many people around here.'

'Famous last words!' Danice whispered. 'Some-one's coming!'

Simon dragged her into a nearby janitor's cupboard. He pulled the door to, leaving a narrow crack to peer through. An agonising few seconds went by. Then there was a noise like an electric blender.

A small motorised robot approached the security barrier. It reached out with a prosthetic hand attached to one of its metal arms and placed it on the handprint reader. The other arm supported a tray which held a steaming mug of tea.

'Cute waiter,' Danice whispered, stealing a look.

'Are you ready to run? We'll probably have a second or two to get through the doors after the robot passes through.'

The thick metal doors parted and slid back in their grooves. The robot moved on.

'Follow it—now!' Simon hissed, dashing for the doors as they reached their maximum opening point.

He pushed all his weight against one door, let Danice slip by and then threw himself through the narrowing gap. The doors shut with a grinding clunk.

'*Whew*, tight fit!' Simon gasped. He looked around and saw that they were standing in a brightly lit corridor.

'It went this way!' Danice said, following a red line that turned to the right around the next corner.

'We're heading straight to the reactor control room,' Simon said, checking the plan of the station on his wrist pilot. 'We're close to it now.'

Danice stopped to peer cautiously around the corner. She nodded back at Simon. He came and took a peek. They were looking into a room that was alight with a bank of fluoro lights. The room contained a control desk in front of a long wall that bristled with gauges, dials and screens. They monitored every aspect of the station's production and output.

'Our objective is to check if there's power going from here to the Chieftain's place,' Simon murmured, stepping slowly into the room. 'Where's that robot got to?'

'Hopefully it's not programmed to raise alarms,' Danice said.

'I doubt it,' Simon replied. 'It looked like some kind of service robot. It probably has pretty basic programming.'

As they reached the control desk, Simon flicked his eyes to the right. Beyond a glass window, a white-coated technician was sitting in a staff recreation area, his back to them as he stirred his tea.

'The robot's in there, I guess. Keeping that guy company,' Danice said.

Simon turned back to the control panels. 'The power outputs are along here,' he said, pointing to a row of gauges marked CITY, FARMS, SOUTH. 'Looks like the station provides power to these places. Those farms must be those Prison Farms you were telling us about.'

Danice nodded. 'That's where the Tribunes send anyone they don't like. Such as people who break into their power plant.'

Simon frowned. 'The power consumption looks pretty low at the Prison Farms.'

Danice pointed to the last gauge. 'The Chieftain's fortress is in the south.'

'Look at the output on that gauge!' Simon exclaimed. 'There's a lot of power going that way right now. Twice as much as to the other places.'

'The Chieftain's probably charging up his Time Accelerator,' Danice said. 'He always starts it a few hours before he needs it—sometimes a day before, if it's a big mission. The further back in time we go, the longer he charges it.'

'So he's preparing for another gold grab?'

'If he's using that much power, he must be.'

'Then that's our next move. South.'

'Back through the city,' Danice said, 'with just one stop.'

'Where?' Simon asked. 'We have to stick to our

orders. They don't like us going off on wild-goose chases.'

'Our stop's on the way. I want to see my dad.'

'I wish I could see my dad,' Simon said, without thinking.

'Why can't you?'

Simon hesitated, then came out with the truth. 'He's dead.'

'I'm sorry,' Danice replied. 'How did he die?'

For a second, Simon considered telling her about the secret investigation into his father's disappearance. But it was too risky. 'I don't want to talk about it,' he said. 'Come on, let's go and find your dad.'

20

'**B**igdad!' Danice cried. She stood on her toes and threw her arms around her father's shoulders.

'Danice! You're back!' her father said in astonishment. He wrapped his great arms around her, casting a curious look over her head at Simon. 'Come on, you and your friend had better get inside.'

'Bigdad, this is Simon,' Danice said, as the door closed behind them. 'Simon, this is Bigdad.'

'Hi,' Simon said, looking up at the giant of a man. He was someone his own father would have described as 'nearly seven foot on the old scale'. He was a complete contrast to Danice's tiny-framed mother.

'Some people call me David,' he said with a wide smile. 'Come, sit down. I've been worried. Where have you been, what have you been up to?'

They sat on wooden chairs in the poorly furnished kitchen. In the following half hour, Danice showed

Bigdad the travel suit under her overalls, described her capture by the Time Bureau in sixteenth century Spain, gave a run-down of her basic training as a temponaut and explained the Bureau's offer to help the family. She finished with their arrival and escape from the Big Forest that morning.

Bigdad turned to Simon. 'And tell me, you're from where?'

'Bondi Beach. You know, Sydney, Australia in the twenty-first century,' he replied, wondering if that really explained anything at all. The beach, surfing and high school seemed so alien and far away.

The explanation seemed to satisfy Bigdad, however. He nodded. 'And what exactly is your mission here?'

Simon hesitated.

'It's okay,' Danice reassured him. 'Bigdad works in the Underground. You can tell him.'

'I'm not sure that's a good idea,' Simon said. 'Our mission plans are confidential.'

'Simon, this is my father!'

Bigdad smiled. 'Perhaps I can reassure you, Simon. The Underground is a group of people working to fight the Tribunes and their political system,' he explained, pointing at a rough wooden shelf holding a few dozen well-worn books. 'Some of us can still read. We know something about the freedoms of the past and we want to get rid of the slave system, establish schools, and change our way of life.'

'We're not allowed to live here with him,' Danice said, with a sad glance at her father.

'It's against regulations for slaves to live with their families,' Bigdad added.

'Couldn't you escape?' Simon asked.

'Yes, I could, very easily, like a lot of the others. But I can be more effective here, in the city.' Bigdad smiled at Simon. 'And we'll help you, too, if we can.'

'Thanks, but Danice and I can't reveal the details of our mission,' Simon said.

'What do you mean?' Danice said. 'Who do you think he's going to talk to? The Tribunes? Bigdad puts his life on the line all the time. He——'

'Danice, it's all right,' Bigdad interrupted.

'No, it's not,' Danice replied, glaring at Simon. 'I'm telling you we can trust Bigdad.'

'Okay, take it easy,' Simon said. He glanced curiously at the big man. He seemed confident, honest and reliable. But Simon and Danice had been instructed not to reveal the complete details of the mission. 'Well . . . er . . .' he muttered, 'we just have to find out a bit about the Chieftain and his time-travel system.'

Danice nodded. 'The Chieftain's powering up his Time Accelerator right now,' she said.

'He's after more gold to keep the Tribunes happy,' Bigdad sighed. 'That's a thankless task. No matter how much you give them, it's never enough, and they'll always demand more.'

'We're supposed to discover the exact location of his Time Accelerator,' Simon said, 'and find out who he really is. Danice says she's never seen him, face to face.'

'I've been into his throne room a couple of times, but he keeps his face always hidden under a hood.' Danice shuddered. 'He's such a creepy man.'

'I've never seen him either,' Bigdad said, 'but the Tribunes have. I hear they say he's an old man. His set-up is basically just him and that sidekick of his, O'Bray.'

'And a whole lot of tough guards,' Danice reminded him.

'Well, first things first,' Bigdad said. 'You'll be hungry. Let's find you something to eat.' He stood up and went to a small bench in the corner. 'You know, maybe the Underground *can* help you. We could create a distraction or two in the city to keep the Tribunes busy—and keep the Chieftain and his guards worried. Keep their minds on other things.'

'Like what?' Danice asked.

Bigdad smiled. 'It won't be hard for us to stir up some unrest. We've had plans for some time to challenge the Tribunes. Our followers in the Underground are keen to make some sort of statement—to shake things up a little, make trouble, show them that we're not completely cowed.'

'If it helps, I guess trouble sounds good,' Simon said.

Danice frowned. 'I don't know, Bigdad. We wouldn't want anyone getting hurt because of us.'

'No one need get hurt,' Bigdad assured her.

'But we're supposed to keep a low profile on these missions,' Danice said. 'Not make disturbances. Not affect history.'

'Leave it to me,' Bigdad said. 'We know how to kick up a fuss without bringing the place down.' He grabbed a half loaf of bread and started slicing it. 'Anyway, you two should stay here till daybreak. It'll take a while for me to start organising things. No point you heading off before we've got the distractions underway!'

'We've only got forty-eight hours' mission time,' Simon said.

Danice yawned. 'A bit of sleep will be good for us.'

Simon felt a surge of weariness, too. 'Okay. But we'd better get moving before dawn. We've still got a lot of objectives to tick off our list before we go back.'

In the darkness, Damien crawled out of the city's waste tunnel, closed the grille behind him and crept up the embankment. He took care to avoid the rivers of sludge running into the drain. The city was quiet, and, after the events of the day, the thought of resting a while in Bigdad's house seemed like the promise of paradise.

He slipped across the open ground, then headed slowly and warily up the alley. Then he flinched as a scavenging rat gave a sharp squeak, leapt from a pile of rubbish and scuttled away.

'Stay steady, stay easy,' he murmured to himself. 'Just a rat.'

Suddenly a gruff voice called out. 'Halt! Stop there!'

Four burly men stepped out of the shadows of a doorway. Damien tensed. He looked around for an escape route.

'Don't even think about it,' the gruff man said, grabbing Damien by the elbow. 'We've been looking for you. The Chieftain wants to see you. Right now!'

21

The 16th Century, Sumatra

The gleaming beach and the green jungle beyond baked in the tropical sun.

Nick stood by the waterline, his hand resting against the shattered hull of the once-mighty Portuguese carrack, the *Coelho do Mar*. 'Wow, big ship!' he said.

The massive carrack had broken into two sections and looked like a whale stranded on the long white beach. Her bow was buried in the sand, and the breakers pounded against the timber planking of her stern, slowly reducing it to wreckage.

'She weighed four hundred tonnes,' Taylor said, lifting her feet carefully as she made her way through a tangle of torn sails, rigging and smashed spars. 'She beached here and broke up when the typhoon hit.'

Ivan pointed to a jagged reef of wave-washed rocks further out in the bay. 'There would have been trouble offshore, too. The ship probably crashed into those rocks and then ended up here.'

Taylor suddenly pointed to where the white body of a sailor lay at the shoreline. A black crab sat on his sea-wrinkled face and picked at his eyes with its claws. 'I wish I hadn't seen that,' she muttered.

Nick crouched into ankle-deep water. 'Hey, I can see a coin!' he yelled.

'There's another one!' Taylor said.

Ivan waded through the water towards her. Shiny, newly minted coins glinted like exotic shells all over the sandy sea-bottom. 'They're everywhere! Thousands of them!' he cried.

'The boxes they were in must have burst open,' Taylor observed. 'It'll take us hours to collect them. And we don't have that much time.'

'Not if those other guys are after this stuff, too,' Nick said.

'Look, let's just focus on our immediate goal,' Ivan said. 'Our mission is to find this gold as quickly as we can, bury it, and make sure it doesn't get transported to the twenty-fourth century.'

'We should look inside the ship,' Nick said, stepping into the gaping hole where the ship had broken its back and split in two. 'There'll be piles of treasure in here somewhere.' He pushed a mangled timber beam out of the way. 'Watch out for splinters!'

Ivan and Taylor followed him cautiously into the gloomy interior of the hull. The fractured cross-section of the stricken ship loomed above them. Amidst the piles of ruptured timber, they could make out the top deck of the aftcastle and the decks beneath.

Nick pointed. 'Up there! That has to be the remains of the captain's cabin. That's gotta be the place to look for gold.'

'So where are the other sailors?' Taylor asked. 'There's no way I want to find any more cold, clammy corpses!'

'Probably out there,' Ivan said. He nodded towards the open sea. 'Or maybe they escaped in the ship's lifeboats.'

'Another coin! Heads, we go up into the cabin; tails, we go out along the beach.' Nick flicked the coin into the air.

'Up!' Ivan said, snatching the coin in midair. 'The only way is up. We have to find that gold. As much as we can carry!'

Simon and Danice made their way through Old City in the early-morning light. Dogs growled in the doorways of the tumbledown shacks. Shabbily dressed locals shuffled past them in the narrow streets, deliberately avoiding eye contact.

'Here we are at the city limits,' Danice said as they stepped into a stretch of open ground between the houses and the city wall. It was fifty metres wide, covered with dry, brown grass and strewn with rubbish.

'Nice spot for a picnic,' Simon remarked.

'Used to be a park. No one looks after it any more,' Danice said. 'That's the security gate down there.'

The gate was about three hundred metres away. A swarm of uniformed guards was closely checking a long line of people and horsedrawn carts as they went through.

'That doesn't look good. Should we go the other way?' Simon said.

Danice shook her head. 'There's another gate around the corner. There are gates about every kilometre.'

'And all heavily guarded, I guess.'

Danice nodded. 'We have to get over the wall, somewhere along here. The Chieftain's place is further south, along the cliffs. It's about twenty minutes' walk.'

'This is the quickest way?' Simon asked.

'Yes. But it's a big leap over,' Danice replied.

Simon moved into the shade of a scrubby tree, one of only a few left growing in the park. He looked up at the wall. It was about ten metres high, made of brick and roughly hewn stone. Loops of razor wire decorated the top, like shiny curls of steel hair.

'We've leapt close to that height before,' Simon said. 'Have we got any other choice?'

'Nope.'

'What's on the other side?'

'Open space like this, I think. Some patches of

small trees, bushes and rocks just beyond that. We can take cover in there, and then make our way to the Chieftain's fortress.'

They activated their wrist pilots, then stepped back a few paces, before checking no one was watching. Then they leapt forward, hitting the ground with their feet together and springing into the air.

Their initial jump over the wall went well, but as they somersaulted over the top, a muddy brown reservoir pond instantly came into view below.

They hadn't trained for water landings, and they bombed into the reservoir, arms and legs flailing. Simon's legs buckled and the air was knocked out of his lungs. The thick overalls dragged him under the surface of the water and into the weed-tangled depths. For a second he thought he would black out, but with a final effort he kicked himself free and struggled to the surface.

'*Ahh . . . ahh!*' he gasped, his lungs sucking in fresh air. He swam the few strokes to the edge and looked around for Danice. She was gripping the stonework that bordered the reservoir, panting and gasping for breath, too.

'You didn't mention there'd be water!' Simon said, trying to get his brain functioning again.

Danice nodded towards the edge of the pond behind him. Simon turned his head and looked straight at a pair of black, size-twelve boots.

'Good morning, sir,' a voice rasped. 'You're under arrest!'

Simon looked up into the metal-pierced face of the meanest-looking man he had ever seen.

The small army shovel dug again and again into the soft white sand.

'I've never buried treasure before,' Nick said, wiping a gritty hand across his dripping forehead. 'How deep would pirates dig?'

The equatorial heat was getting to him and he was thinking there were better places to be than at the bottom of a big hole.

'That's deep enough,' Taylor said, dropping a chunky gold statue of a tiger onto the sand.

Four statues now stood in a row, alongside a chest of coins and a stack of two hundred solid gold finger bars.

'If this is only part of that Malaccan rajah's treasure, he must have been some rich dude,' Nick said.

'Let's just hide it and get back to somewhere with proper airconditioning,' Ivan said, checking his wrist pilot. 'Our TPS will be here any minute.'

'So, did you guys find all the gold?' Nick stopped work and stood up in the hole. Only his head showed above the ground. 'Or have you been slacking off while I've been slaving my guts out?'

'This is everything that was easy to get,' Taylor

said, glancing back to the wreck of the *Coelho do Mar*. 'We were told not to take risks.'

'There's nothing left on the ship that we could see.' Ivan tossed a canvas bag to the ground. It clinked loudly. 'But I picked up some of the coins that spilled into the water.'

'Okay, it's just this lot then,' Taylor said. She lay down, grasped Nick's arm and helped him out of the hole.

As soon as he was clear, Ivan shoved in one of the heavy gold statues. It hit the bottom with a thud.

Nick picked up one of the other statues. 'You know, I reckon the prof's wrong. We should take some of this gold back with us. It would be worth a quid or two.'

'We can't,' Taylor said. 'The local people are supposed to find most of this gold over the next couple of months. Our orders are to bury it. Not to change things.'

'I know! I know! A time traveller goes back to see the dinosaurs, accidentally kills a butterfly and changes the whole course of history,' Nick drawled.

'You could argue we've done that anyway,' Ivan said. 'The villagers will find this treasure only because we put it here.'

'Or you could argue that it was going to end up here all along, whether we did it or not,' Nick replied.

'All we really know is that it will be found,' Ivan stated.

'Guys, cut the time-paradox talk!' Taylor said. 'The satellite's here!'

A few metres up the beach, the air broke into a swirling vortex as their TPS materialised.

'We've got about ten minutes,' Taylor said. 'Bury it!'

They toiled under the baking sun. Ivan and Taylor pushed all the gold into the hole and Nick layered the sand on top. Within seven minutes it was done, and Nick smoothed the sand flat with the frond of a palm tree.

'There,' he said, proudly eyeing his handiwork. 'No one will know we've ever been here.'

'Only them!' Taylor said, pointing to a second wormhole that had begun to appear beside the shipwreck. 'We can't let them see us.'

'Drop everything!' Ivan said. He ran up the beach and dived into their own exit tunnel.

Taylor quickly followed.

'There goes easy money!' Nick said. He tossed the frond away and leapt into the void himself.

Alongside the *Coelho do Mar*, the other TPS entered the timezone in a swirl of colours. Damien and Lee materialised on the beach.

'Looks like we've found it!' Damien said, stretching his arms and legs back to life. He held up a hand, shading his face from the hot sun.

'Wow, big ship!' Lee said, goggling at the wreck.

'Come on, we can't stand around staring,' Damien said. 'There's a village up the coast. We better get this gold before anyone else does, or else the Chieftain will be really mad at us!'

22

'**Y**OWWW! That hurts. It doesn't peel straight off, you know!' Simon protested, as a black-moustached Security Officer plucked hard at the fabric of his time-travel suit. In fact, he wanted to tell the man it *did* peel off. But not like this. You needed to wallow in a bath of dissolving chemicals for a couple of hours to do it right, and without causing pain.

'I'll ask you one final time,' the officer snarled. 'Why wear this under your overalls?'

'I like to wear a lot of clothes. I feel the cold,' Simon replied.

'Where did you get this strange outfit? Who gave it to you? It looks like a uniform. Who are you really working for?'

'Who are *you* working for?' Simon muttered.

'You only need to know that I'm paid to pick up vermin like you!'

Simon tapped the toe of his right foot nervously.

The continual questioning was getting to him. Mainly because no amount of telling outright lies, or staring out through the window and refusing to answer, seemed to be helping him. Not only that, the questioning was getting monotonous and exhausting.

'And what's this?' the officer demanded, indicating Simon's wrist pilot.

For that, at least Simon could come up with some kind of true answer. 'It's like a watch, a calculator, a calendar,' he said. 'All in one. Can't take it off, sorry. It's built into the suit.'

'Mmm, very sophisticated piece of work. For a watch!'

Simon's foot continued to tap on the floor.

'Okay, we'll go over this again,' the stout officer said. 'You say you're a bicycle courier. Which is why you're wearing this strange suit.'

'That's it.'

'Liar!' The officer glared at him. 'The only bicycle you'll find within ten kilometres of this place is in the Old City Museum! There is no such thing as a bicycle courier!'

Again, Simon tried to avoid a direct answer. 'But I *can* ride a bike, you know.'

'You also tell me you're on a clandestine training program for our armed forces!'

'That's why I can't talk about it. It's a secret.'

The officer poked a stubby finger hard into Simon's chest. '*Pah*, lies! Tell me the truth and save yourself trouble. For the last time, who are you and why are you here?'

Simon shrugged. Maybe he should tell some of the truth.

'Okay,' he said. 'My name's Simon Savage. I'm a temponaut. That's a time traveller from the twenty-first century. I work for the Time Bureau and I've come here to learn about your culture and technology.'

The officer sucked in a deep breath. He looked like a cane toad suddenly inflated with air. 'Time traveller . . . twenty-first . . . century!' he spluttered.

'It's true!' Simon cried.

The man leaned forward and grabbed Simon by the side of his neck. 'You think I'm stupid. That I couldn't find a maggot on a dead sheep or a flea on a dog!'

'I . . . didn't . . . say that,' Simon said, choking with the pressure from the man's hand.

'*Pah!*' The man let go and stepped back.

Simon rubbed his neck.

'I'm being easy on you, Savage, or whatever your name is,' the man said. 'But the Tribunes have other people who can extract this information from you. Tougher people, much more brutal than me.' His beady eyes flicked to a neighbouring room. 'And your friend might be in danger from them right at this moment. On the other hand, she might be telling us the truth.'

'Danice . . . is she all right?' Simon asked.

'Cooperate and I might be able to tell you.'

Simon stared out the window again. What could he say? Nothing worked with this guy. He didn't believe the lies, and he didn't believe the truth either.

'Perhaps you think silence might work,' the officer said. 'Okay, so I'll give you time to think about your story. Think about what you want to tell me.'

He pressed the red buzzer on his desk. The mean-looking guard from the pond entered the room and saluted.

'Take him away!' the officer snarled. Then, as if having a new thought, he smiled. 'Take him to the Pit!'

Danice heard a man laughing in the next room. She looked towards the connecting door, then back at the solemn face of her interrogator. This was a slim, dark-haired female officer in a smart blue uniform.

'So you continue to insist you're a time traveller, from the twenty-first century?' the woman repeated for the fifth time.

'That's right,' Danice replied patiently.

'Which you say explains this strange outfit you're wearing. But your story is too fanciful. It's the story of a child, the sort of thing you probably heard in a fairytale. Not something that happens in the real world. You'll have to come up with something better.'

Danice realised that the woman had no idea Danice was actually a local forest-dweller. Her time-travel suit had put the woman off the scent and was as good as a disguise. But Danice wondered what the woman actually did know. Did she know about the Chieftain's time-travel missions? Did she know where or how he got his gold? Apparently not, but Danice was more worried about revealing even the slightest clue that she had a family living in the Big Forest, and a father who slaved away in the city. She had to protect them, and the safest course was to keep distracting this woman.

'But maybe time travel does happen here. Maybe it does happen in this time. Have you ever thought about that?' Danice said.

The woman smiled thinly. 'Go ahead and think these fanciful notions, if you want to, but they don't interest me.' She stood up. 'Still, maybe we can jog the truth from you in other ways. A little time at the Prison Farms might be good for you.'

Danice groaned inwardly. That would be the worst fate of all. If she went to the Farms she would never be heard of again.

'But they don't send kids to the Farms,' she said, without thinking.

The woman pounced. 'And how do you know that?' she demanded. 'You seem very knowledgeable about our society, for a newcomer. For someone who says they're a stranger.'

'Um, it just sounds bad, real bad,' Danice said quickly. 'A prison farm, I mean.'

'It's worse than you can imagine,' the officer said. 'I suggest you think long and hard about your story. And think about how long you'll survive out there at the Farms! Someone will be along soon to take you to the Pit.'

She turned and left Danice alone in the room.

23

The Pit was aptly named. It was a deep, damp and miserable dogbox carved into the solid rock in the courtyard of the City Prison. The top of the Pit was open to the sky through a grate of thick metal bars. Simon sat on a slimy block of stone and stared up at a sun that gave little comfort at that depth below ground.

At least his suit insulated him from the cold. He tried not to flinch at every drop of water that fell on his head, or at the scuffle of every creature scuttling in the dark corners. The black cockroaches were giants. He had spotted one over eight centimetres long—bigger than the ones that crawled around their Sydney kitchen in summer.

Simon wondered if his situation could get any worse. He was imprisoned in a hole, stranded in a time that wasn't his own, in a country he didn't know. And he was separated both from Danice and the timeline back home. The mission was on the verge of being a failure. No one would ever know who the Chieftain was, or what had happened to Simon. He would never get back to his own time. He would probably die, right there in a pit in the twenty-fourth century.

Simon buried his face in his hands.

Suddenly there was a cry from above. 'Simon! Simon!'

The grate was lifted by a burly guard, and a moment later, Danice was shoved down the slippery metal ladder.

Simon jumped to his feet. 'Danice! Are you okay?'

'Yeah, I'm all right,' she replied. '*Phew!* This place really is the pits!'

Simon's spirits were already lifting. 'It's quiet and there's plenty of running water,' he said.

'What about spiders?'

'No. But cockroaches and lizards, yes.'

Danice shuddered. 'That's all right, then. I hate spiders, especially when you can't get away from them.'

'Did they give you the third degree?' Simon asked. 'What did you tell them?'

'That I was a time traveller from the twenty-first century. They didn't believe me.'

Simon smiled. 'Funny, I tried that one, too.'

'Didn't work?'

'We're in here, aren't we?'

'Okay, so what are we going to do?'

Simon shrugged. 'No one knows we're here and no one knows we're in trouble. Not your family, not the Time Bureau, no one.'

'We're on our own,' Danice agreed.

'And we're a long way from the TPS rendezvous point,' Simon added.

'Not much future at the bottom of a pit,' Danice murmured.

'I don't see how we're going to get out of this dump,' Simon said.

'And I'm starving.'

Simon patted the empty travel pouch on the right thigh of his suit. 'Did they take your food bars from you, too?' he asked.

Danice nodded ruefully.

Simon looked around at the slimy dark walls. 'How long do you think they'll keep us here?'

'Somehow, I don't think it's going to be long.'

'Why do you say that?'

'They're just leaving us here to soften us up. I think they're planning to send us away.' Danice made a face. 'In fact, I'm pretty sure they are sending us away.'

'Where?'

'One place we don't want to be. The Prison Farms!'

'Ah, *porcus*! Please try the *porcus*, gentlemen,' the Chieftain said.

He indicated the roast suckling pig that O'Bray had placed in the centre of the dining table. On each side of this new platter were solid gold bowls, filled with fresh fruits, nuts, cheeses and fresh bread rolls. 'And please do try these baked dormice, dipped in honey and rolled in poppy seeds!'

'A true Roman banquet. Extraordinary!' one of his three guests said.

Tyrone was a stern man with an ugly scar furrowing his left cheek. He brushed a few bread-crumbs from his red silk shirt, and then took a baked dormouse between a thumb and forefinger, lifted it into his mouth and crushed the creature's tiny bones between his teeth. 'Mmm, absolutely delicious!' he said, licking his lips. 'This is like something described in the history books—the food extolled by the poets of old.'

The Chieftain chuckled. 'Well, I'm a great fan of the poets of old.'

'It certainly beats the dull fare we usually have for lunch,' Cyrus said. He was a hunched man with big hands like crab claws. He leaned forward to spear a roast pigeon with his fork and dumped it on his plate. 'We're lucky if we get good meat and fresh vegetables three times a week.'

'How do you manage all this?' Magnus enquired. He had tanned, leathery skin and the steel-grey eyes of a carnivorous lizard. He eyed the gold dishes and cutlery with envy, and tried to hide his curiosity. The Chieftain's ability to acquire wealth, fine foods and wine was a constant mystery to him.

The Chieftain eased back in his chair and looked thoughtfully at his three guests. They were the Tribunes, the much-feared rulers of Old City. Men whom he disliked and held in complete contempt, though he would never admit this out loud, even to O'Bray.

'It takes hard work, gentlemen,' he said. 'When you've been trading and travelling as long as I have, you make contacts. And gold always helps. Speaking of which, there will be the usual gifts for you gentlemen to take home with you today.'

The Chieftain nodded to O'Bray, who hurried across the room to a covered trolley. 'O'Bray, if you please!' the Chieftain ordered.

O'Bray bowed, and then with an exaggerated flourish, whipped away a fine, embroidered cloth to reveal three piles. Each pile contained fifty gold finger bars, three golden horn-shaped beakers and three baskets of gold coins.

The Tribunes gasped in unison.

'Trinkets from antiquity for you to do with as you please,' the Chieftain said. He clicked his fingers. 'Bring them over, O'Bray, let my friends get a closer look.'

As O'Bray pushed the trolley towards the table,

Tyrone whispered to his lizard-like neighbour, 'Did you hear that? He thinks we're his friends.'

Cyrus smiled, turned to the Chieftain, and pointed to the trolley. 'These golden horns, they're superb.'

'I believe they're from a medieval castle in Bulgaria,' the Chieftain said vaguely.

Unable to keep their hands off their gifts, the Tribunes rose from their chairs and began to inspect the gold on the trolley.

'If I may have a word with you, boss,' O'Bray murmured in his ear.

The Chieftain excused himself, left the table and followed O'Bray to the far side of his reception room. O'Bray glanced over his shoulder, ensuring the Tribunes could not hear their conversation. 'Firstly, your guests sent their thugs on a raid into the forest today. To your part of the forest.'

'I saw the airships passing over.' The Chieftain gritted his teeth. 'And after I pay them so well to stay off my patch.'

'They go where they like,' O'Bray muttered, eyes to the ground. 'Just to exercise their power.'

'Just to show they can,' the Chieftain added.

'And secondly . . . the mission to Sumatra has failed.'

'How could that happen? We planned it so carefully!'

O'Bray hesitated. He hated delivering bad news. The Chieftain would sink into a foul mood, and worse, he would take away the bonus that O'Bray had come to enjoy after every successful mission. But there was no holding back what he had to say.

'Damien reported that most of the gold was already gone,' O'Bray said. 'He and Lee found only a few kilos of coins that had spilled into the sea. They bagged the coins and brought them back, so we do have something for our efforts. But the bulk of the treasure had already disappeared.'

'This is a disaster!'

'I'm sorry, boss.'

'Sorry won't do, O'Bray,' the Chieftain snarled. 'How am I supposed to maintain this fortress, pay the guards, and pay for the power I need for our missions? How do you expect me to keep paying the Tribunes?'

'There's something else,' O'Bray said, ignoring the Chieftain's outburst.

'Very well, I'm waiting.'

'I was outside earlier, talking to one of the Tribune's top men. A man we often pay for information.' O'Bray's black eyes narrowed. 'It seems that two strangers, two young people in bizarre uniforms, have been captured outside Old City.'

'And why would this interest me?' the Chieftain snapped.

O'Bray kept his voice down. 'It's their appearance. They were disguised in overalls, but wearing a type of thick bodysuit underneath. From what my source told me, and from what I can work out, they're something like the travel suits you supply to Damien and the others.'

The Chieftain nodded thoughtfully.

'But there's more. One of their security people reported that both these youngsters said they were time travellers. The security man joked about it, but . . . well, I thought you might like to know.'

The Chieftain frowned. 'An interesting remark. Even if it was a joke.'

'Exactly what I thought, boss.'

The Chieftain glanced at his guests. They were so busy pawing their gold that they didn't seem to notice their host's absence. 'Do the Tribunes know about this yet?'

O'Bray shook his head. 'No. They will find out soon, but no one wants to interrupt their entertainment right now.'

'Well, find out more about these travellers. Find out all you can,' the Chieftain said quietly. He gave O'Bray a curt nod and returned to the table. 'Eat up, gentlemen!' he cried expansively. 'Have some more wine. Go ahead, enjoy yourselves. Please!'

24

The airship jolted as it came to a halt at the end of a half-hour journey across the Big Forest. Footsteps pounded and voices yelled outside as the ship was secured to the docking tower.

'Stand up, you two!' a black-uniformed guard barked.

'I guess this is it,' Simon said, getting to his feet.

Danice rose with him and together they stepped to a window and looked out.

'Doesn't look much like a farm,' Simon said.

Below, there were dozens of factory-like buildings, with large, cleared patches of land beyond. The entire compound was enclosed by yet another monumental razor-wire fence that stretched for kilometres to the north and south.

'Move out!' the guard ordered.

'Where do they get the wire for all these fences?' Danice muttered.

'What difference does it make?' Simon shrugged, stepping from the doorway of the airship onto the docking tower. 'The fences are either keeping us out, or keeping us in.'

'Down the steps!' the guard directed them.

'Where are we going?' Simon asked.

'You'll find out soon enough,' the man replied.

At the bottom of the tower, they were pushed through a gate, across a yard, through a door, and then into a poorly lit office. The air in the room was stale and stank of stewed coffee and burnt food. A messy stove and a pile of grubby pans in one corner suggested that this was where the smells came from . . . until Simon spotted a plump unshaven man in a uniform so stained and dirty that it looked like he might be the main source of the rank odours. The man peered at them over the top of his spectacles and waved towards the far wall. 'Take a seat. You'll be dealt with soon!'

As Simon and Danice made their way to a wooden bench, a phone rang. The officer picked it up.

'Yes, Tribune. They're both here now,' he said. 'Oh, I see, spies, eh? What, from England, Europe?'

'We're spies now?' Simon whispered.

'They probably think we've been spies all along,' Danice said.

'I suppose we are, in a way,' Simon murmured.

'Yes, I see,' the man said. 'They're too much trouble . . . Very well, I'll deal with it, Tribune . . .

Yes, don't worry.' He hung up. 'So, what am I to do with you two, eh?' he said, turning to grin at them.

'Well, sir, we'd be happy to leave. Any time,' Simon said. He sounded much braver than he felt.

'Shut up!' the officer grunted. 'It's your job to stay quiet and do as you're told.' He grinned again to show his broken teeth. 'You're going to provide us with entertainment.'

'What do you mean?' Simon asked.

The official ignored Simon and rang the bell on his desk. A guard opened the door and stepped in.

'Take these two *spies* to the main cell block,' the officer barked. 'And have the pond prepared for tomorrow morning.' He stood up and rubbed his hands gleefully. 'At seven a.m. you will assemble the prison population for one of our little shows.'

The guard couldn't conceal his excitement. 'Another show? Great! Yes, sir!' he said, with a beaming smile. 'We'll be ready, sir!'

Simon turned to Danice. 'What pond? And what do they mean by entertainment?'

'I've never heard of ponds or entertainment around here,' she replied. 'But it sounds bad.'

'I don't think they like us much,' Simon said as they were manhandled outside.

On the Time Bureau's tracking screen, the two red dots pulsed south-west of Old City.

'What are Simon and Danice doing out there?' Captain Cutler wondered. 'They're supposed to be in the city, or near the Chieftain's fortress.'

Harry studied the vision stream from the twenty-fourth century. 'No idea, sir. Once you get off the cliff escarpment, there's a huge area of the Big Forest, west and south of the city. Simon and Danice are in a position even further south, about thirty k's from the city, in a cleared section of the forest. It looks like some sort of agricultural zone. We think there may be farms there that supply the city with food.'

'And what is Simon and Danice's status?'

'They're stationary at that location.'

'Very well,' Cutler said. 'We should prepare to move the TPS and the timeline to this new position. Time's running out for this mission and they might need quick access.'

'I'll have it readied.'

Cutler stared thoughtfully at the screen.

'Anything else, sir?' Harry asked.

'We should have Nick, Taylor and Ivan put on mission standby.'

'You sure, sir? They haven't had their Down Time,' Harry said.

'They're fit and young,' Cutler replied. 'I'll get the medical staff to give them boosters. And they can have double Down Time on their return.'

Harry glanced with concern at the captain. 'Are you worried, sir?'

Cutler nodded. 'There's the possibility our two young temponauts are in trouble. What sort of trouble I don't know. But we had better be ready for anything. It is essential this mission succeeds.'

Damien sipped a cup of hot tea and listened as his father addressed a gathering of the Underground members in the basement of his house.

'Welcome! I'm glad we've all managed to get here at such short notice,' Bigdad said. 'And I'm glad our organisers could make it, because I think it's time for some positive action.'

'Yes! Yes!' a few voices replied.

A young woman got to her feet. She wore a determined look on her face. 'Do you mean we should proceed with our plans to steal the airship?'

'Action has been on our minds for a while now,' Bigdad went on. 'We've often discussed how we need to contact the people in the Far Lands. We've all heard stories about their freedoms, and of how they govern themselves. And also of how they're willing to help other people achieve freedom, too.'

There were murmurs of assent around the room.

'But before we make any further plans, we need to find out if the stories are true. And visiting the Far Lands is the best way to do it.'

'That's why we've been keeping an eye on that docking tower in the north of the city,' the young woman said. 'It has the smallest troop of guards, and we know their routine down to the last minute. We know when to strike!'

The room broke into applause.

'Then this is our plan,' Bigdad said, indicating a bearded man in a woollen cap. 'Peter will gather together as many people as he can and stir up some unrest in the city plaza.'

The bearded man nodded in reply.

'Just enough to distract the Tribunes,' Bigdad elaborated, 'and to get them to commit a few hundred soldiers and guards to control the situation. While that happens, I'll take a smaller party up to the docking tower—and we'll do our best to take that airship.'

'Hear, hear!' a dozen voices replied.

'I'll send word when we're ready to move.'

'Death to the Tribunes!' the bearded man said, leading another round of applause.

The room immediately began to buzz with conversation.

Damien took the opportunity to approach his father. 'I thought you were going to ask if anyone had seen Danice since she and Simon left this morning?'

Bigdad drew him aside. 'I decided it mightn't be wise. Some of them know Danice, but none of them know Simon,' he said, 'and there's no point alarming people with stories of time travellers. Or trying to explain it, for that matter.' He managed a smile.

'Remember, it took months for me to understand what you, Danice and Alli were doing for the Chieftain.'

'We don't have to tell them the whole story,' Damien said. 'We just need to know if Danice is okay!'

'We can't simply say that Simon has appeared out of nowhere,' Bigdad said. 'It's better not to bring up the subject at all.'

Damien scowled. 'If you're not going to do anything, then I'll go and look for her on my own.'

'No, I want you to stay,' Bigdad said. 'I promised Danice I would stir up some trouble and hopefully keep some attention away from her and her friend while they do what they have to.' He shrugged. 'Whether it will work, I don't know.' He put a reassuring hand on Damien's shoulder. 'But our plan serves two purposes. We need to take this airship in any case, and to do that, I need your support. Stay for now, please. By staying, you'll be helping Danice in the long run.'

The night closed in and a misty rain drifted down on the cell block. Simon stared out through the barred window and watched the bright droplets dance in the searchlights that constantly moved across the walls outside.

He had been thinking about escape from the moment they'd been locked in. But the cell block was constructed of solid stone and steel, and it would take heavy tools, if not a bulldozer, to make so much as a mark on the walls.

'Fat chance,' he muttered to himself. 'There's no way out of here.'

Danice sat on the top bunk. Her face was only just visible in the light from outside. 'Simon, it's not your fault, you know,' she said. 'We both got caught and neither of us made a mistake. So don't blame yourself, okay?'

Simon was silent.

'Okay?' Danice insisted.

'I just didn't expect we'd end up here,' Simon said, 'and the TPS is due back tomorrow morning.'

'I guess we'll miss that,' Danice said.

Simon paced away from the window and back again. 'I keep thinking about my mum and sister. I didn't speak to them before we left.' He paused. 'Maybe the Time Bureau will tell them I was lost in action. Or that I died in an accident.'

Danice sighed. 'It's probably better not to think about that.'

'I know! I read the manual,' Simon replied. '*Rule Number Twenty-Seven: in adverse situations, keep a positive outlook.*' He sighed. 'Only it's hard when you're stuck in jail, with no hope of getting out.'

'But the Bureau won't forget us, will they?' Danice asked. 'They know exactly what timezone we're in. We just have to hang in here and wait for them to find us.'

'Except they don't know where we are,' Simon said.

Danice yawned. 'Well, you go ahead and be negative. I'm going to sleep.'

Simon continued to stare gloomily through the bars. But he found no comfort in the rain or the darkness, and there was no hint out there of what the dawn might bring.

25

Harsh bells jangled in Simon's ears. He sprang up and banged his head on the bunk above. *'Owww!'* he cried. He clutched at his skull and felt for any stickiness in his hair.

'You okay?' Danice asked, leaning down.

'Am I bleeding?'

'Not that I can see.'

'What's all the racket?' Simon asked, rubbing his head with one hand and lifting the other to check his wrist pilot. 'It's only four-thirty, local time.'

There was a chorus of muffled yawns and the shuffling of feet throughout the cell block. Simon climbed off the bunk and went to the barred door. In the faint light from the light globes, he could see signs of movement as the occupants stirred in the other cells.

'Must be wake-up time,' Danice said.

'I should have known we'd be up early,' Simon grumbled.

'We have to beat the birds out to the worms,' Danice said lightly.

'Move! Move! Doors!' a voice bellowed.

There was an orchestrated *Clunk!* as each cell door automatically opened.

'Move, you morons!' the voice boomed again. 'Assemble! Now!'

Danice jumped down from the top bunk, and they stepped through the open door into the corridor. As many as a hundred other prisoners were also trooping out of their cells, some still pulling on grimy orange shirts and scuffing their feet into boots. They were well drilled and, just as they had on a thousand other mornings, they automatically turned towards the steel exit door at the end of the corridor and stood, waiting like sheep for it to be opened.

A beefy guard stopped in front of Simon and Danice. 'You two! Stay there!' Short lengths of chain were draped over his shoulder. He gestured to another guard to join him. 'Hey, Jack, give us a hand.'

'What's going on?' Simon protested.

'Shut up and never you mind!' the guard growled.

He shoved Simon against the wall, while the other man shackled his ankles in chains and snapped the linking lock shut.

'The girl, too!'

'Let go of me!' Danice struggled and kicked out at him.

The guard slapped her face.

She gasped with shock.

'You animal!' Simon yelled.

He sprang forward, but the chain between his ankles drew tight and he tripped and fell headlong on the flagstone floor. The beefy guard kicked him in the stomach.

Cheers came from the prisoners in the corridor. They hadn't seen so much fun in months.

'Get them both out of here!' the guard told his workmate.

Simon clambered to his feet and kept his eyes on the ground as he shuffled past the lined-up prisoners. His chains dragged on the ground with each step.

'You okay?' Danice whispered, waddling along next to him in her own chains.

'Just a bit winded. You?'

She rubbed her cheek. 'I'm all right.'

They left the cell block, crossed a yard, then continued on past the last building in the compound and into a grove of small redwoods. On either side of the grassy path, watchful guards in khaki uniforms were posted every twenty metres to prevent thoughts of escape. By the time Simon and Danice reached the far end of the woods, the first rays of sunlight from the east were piercing through the branches and casting faint, rippling shadows on the ground.

The path skirted a small hill, then led to a set of gates into what looked like a sportsground. The far side of the hill had been roughly excavated into an amphitheatre. Several terraces made tiers up to the top, and wooden planks mounted on blocks provided seating for a few hundred people.

The seats faced a circular expanse of greenish-grey water at the foot of the mound, about ten metres in diameter. The surface of the pond seemed to be alive. Dozens of olive-brown, snake-like forms constantly rose in the water, their shovel-shaped mouths sucking in air before they twisted back into the pond.

Danice stopped dead in her tracks, a look of dread on her face. 'What are they?'

'Eels,' the guard said. 'We breed a lot of them out here.'

'What do you want us to do?' Simon asked. 'Fish for them?'

'You'll find out soon enough.' The man turned in the direction of a small shed near the first row of seats. 'Hey, Dan! Dan?'

The shed's rickety door opened and a wiry old man in overalls stepped out. 'Yeah, I'm here!'

The guard nodded at Simon and Danice. 'They're all yours. Get them ready. I'm returning to the block.'

He headed back up the path, leaving Simon and Danice alone with the man called Dan.

Dan squinted, looking them up and down. 'You prisoners are gettin' younger all the time. Hope I've got somethin' that fits you.'

He shuffled back into the shed and, a moment

later, came back with two pairs of thick rubber gloves and two pairs of thigh-high rubber boots. He threw them at Simon and Danice's feet.

Simon picked up a glove and turned it over. It had a rough surface on the palm and on the underside of the fingers. 'What's this for?' he asked.

'Grabbin' eels. And throwin' 'em!'

'Why would we do that?' Danice asked.

'You poor blighters!' Dan jerked a thumb towards the pond. 'They're electric eels in there. They can kill you, if you touch 'em, take my word for it.'

'I'm not touching them!' Simon said. 'Not in a hundred years!'

Dan's eyes flickered quickly to the path to check no one was nearby. 'Look, that's why you're here. For the eel throwin'. It's the only entertainment we've got!'

'What!' Simon and Danice said together.

'It's a contest. One-on-one,' he went on, pushing on a glove to demonstrate. 'The gloves on your hands and the rubber boots on your feet insulate you from electric shocks when you get into the water. You reach in, grab the first eel you find, and then you try to throw it at the other guy before he throws one at you! And those eels sure get angry when you pick 'em up. If one hits you, it'll give off eight hundred volts.'

'Danice and I have to throw them at each other?' Simon asked. 'Like gladiators?'

'That's right! You only need a couple of hundred volts to kill you. These beasts fry you good!' The man looked sadly at Simon and Danice. 'And the last one standin'—if the warden likes 'em, and if they're lucky—they's allowed to live!'

An hour passed and the tiered seats were soon filled with hordes of rowdy prisoners, excited by the prospect of an hour off work. They were mainly men and youths, but Simon also saw about twenty women in their orange prison-issue clothes, all just as eager as the rest of the prisoners for the morning's gladiatorial contest.

The crowd began a slow clap, impatient for the event to start, while dozens of baton-wielding guards kept a wary eye on the gathering.

'So this is what passes for fun around here,' Simon said. He gave his legs a shake now that their chains had been removed. 'Haven't they heard of the movies?'

'They must be mad if they think I'm going to chuck eels at you,' Danice said, 'and try to kill you!'

'Take your gloves!' old Dan interrupted. 'The only advice I can give you youngsters is to throw first and throw often!'

Loud jeers greeted the warden as he stepped out in front of the crowd with a loudhailer.

'Gentlemen, and ladies!' he bellowed, bowing

gracelessly towards the women. 'Welcome to today's contest!'

Cheers greeted his announcement.

The warden's eyes scanned the prisoners seated in the front row. 'In order for today's fight to be a true contest, we'll need two more volunteers! You two will do!' He pointed at two boys in their late teens, then nodded to four guards standing by, who plucked the protesting boys from their seats.

The other prisoners greeted this selection with loud applause.

'Looks like we won't have to fight each other after all,' Simon muttered to Danice.

'Bet we still have to fight,' she replied grimly.

The guards pushed the two teenage boys towards the opposite edge of the pond. The boys glanced nervously at the eels in the water, but seemed to have already accepted their fate as part of the day's entertainment. The taller boy took a look at Simon, summoned up some courage and spat in his direction.

'Quiet!' the warden roared at the crowd. 'Now, it's been a long time since we had any real entertainment out here . . .'

'Yeah—too long!' a voice yelled.

'Take that prisoner's name!' the warden hissed to the guard at his side. 'Give him an extra week on the wheat thresher!'

A chorus of boos greeted the order.

Simon turned to Danice. A loose plan had formed in his mind. 'This fight might be our chance to escape,' he whispered.

'How? Escape by electrocution?'

'First thing, just before the fight starts, we should put our helmets up for extra protection,' Simon said.

He activated his wrist pilot and put it on standby. Danice did the same.

'Do you think our suits will protect us?' she asked.

'Don't know. But the helmet might stop us getting a shock in the face!'

'That warden's speaking again,' Danice warned.

'Good. I'll talk while he does. Then no one will hear what I'm saying.'

'Quiet, you rabble,' the warden growled. 'Or we call the whole thing off!'

An instant hush fell over the crowd.

Simon waited until the warden started bellowing into the loudhailer again, then kept whispering in Danice's ear.

'Today's contest is between these two devious miscreants . . .' the warden said, nodding towards the two teenagers.

There were loud cheers. Encouraged by the crowd's support, the boys now raised their arms with an air of bravado.

'And over here,' the warden said, waving a hand towards Simon and Danice, 'are two youngsters who I'll bet are sorry they ever set eyes on us. And they'll be even sorrier by the time we've finished with them!'

There were boos and catcalls.

'So don't forget . . . wait for my signal,' Simon said under his breath. 'When I say—NOW!'

'Got it,' Danice replied.

The warden slipped a thick rubber glove onto his hand and stepped towards the pond. 'But let's not forget the real stars of our show,' he announced.

With practised skill, he plunged his hand into the water and dragged out a writhing eel, more than a metre long. He held it up. 'These shocking devils carry a violent kick. They are what make this event the special occasion that it is!'

The eel hissed loudly. Suddenly, with no warning, the warden hurled it into the front row of prisoners. Its tail slapped loudly against a man's neck and face, giving off a crackle like a mini lightning bolt.

'*Yaaa!*' the man screeched.

He jerked around like a puppet on strings, his body shaking and his eyes popping. Then he collapsed to the ground.

The prisoners cheered madly.

'They have to be really stirred up to deliver a shock like that!' the warden yelled. 'Who wants to see some more?'

There were more cheers and whistles.

'Then get our contestants ready!'

Guards stepped forward and pushed Simon and

Danice towards the pond. A stocky guard waved his baton menacingly in their faces. 'When I tell ya to get in, ya get in!'

Simon shuffled to the edge with Danice.

'Put the boots on!' the guard said. 'Quick!'

Simon and Danice slipped their feet into the rubber boots that Dan had given them. Their opponents on the other side of the pond did the same. The taller boy glared at Simon and held up the middle finger of his right hand.

Simon gave him an upright clenched fist in reply. As a sportsman, he knew he should try and dominate his opponent from the start.

'All right, take it easy. *Now* put on the gloves,' the guard ordered.

Simon drew them on and exchanged a nervous glance with Danice. 'Just remember our plan,' he said.

'As our competitors approach the Pond of Death,' the warden roared, 'here are the rules of today's contest. When I say, "Go!" each competitor will throw eels at their opponent until one of them drops. Either from exhaustion, or from electrocution!'

'*Woo! Woo!*' the prisoners yelled.

The two teenage boys slapped high fives.

'The young man can go first,' the warden said, pointing to Simon. 'Let the contestants enter the water!'

A guard got behind Simon, shepherding him like a cattle dog.

'He's mine!' the taller boy said, stepping straight into the knee-deep water.

The warden's 'Go!' echoed around the stadium.

Simon stared at the sinuous shapes surging in the water. He knew there was no avoiding this contest. He had no desire to hurt anyone, but he had no alternative. Failure to hurt his opponent meant death or injury to himself. Simon punched his wrist pilot to activate his helmet. With a faint metallic buzz, it covered his head, leaving a transparent visor protecting his eyes, and giving him about twenty minutes' breathing time inside the suit.

'Boo! Make him take it off!' a female prisoner yelled.

Simon ignored her and stepped into the water. He saw a hazy blur of faces on the benches above him.

Six or seven metres away, his rival was already in the pond. He grabbed a thrashing eel and hurled it at Simon's head.

Simon ducked and the eel splashed into the water a metre to his right.

'Boo! Get him off!' a man yelled with all the fervour of a fanatical football spectator.

'Fight on! Fight on!' the warden ordered.

Simon and the boy circled around the edge of the pond.

They kept their distance, their eyes constantly on each other's slightest movement. Like his opponent,

Simon held one hand underwater and kept feeling around for an eel.

'Boo! Boo!' the crowd complained, getting restless.

A grin split the youth's face as he whipped his hand from the water, swung a snapping-mouthed eel around his head and let it go. The eel zipped over the surface of the pond. Simon arched his body to one side to avoid it and slipped on the slimy bottom of the pond. As he fell, he was vaguely aware of the cheers from the prisoners. They thought the eel had brought him down. He reached out with his hands to break his fall, pushed against the bottom of the pond and resurfaced. He struggled to his feet, plunged his hands back into the water and grabbed hold of an eel. He twisted around to confront his opponent, aimed, and then threw the eel with one arm.

The boy took a dive, too, and the eel cartwheeled over his head to land on the ground, flopping and gasping in front of the wildly cheering prisoners.

Then Simon's opponent got to his feet, another eel at the ready. He waded closer and tossed his eel at Simon. The creature's deadly tail flicked the side of Simon's helmet. He heard a crack of electricity and felt a stab of pain through his head. He gasped, but he had no time to think. A dozen frightened eels swirled at his feet. He plunged both his hands into the water and clasped onto one.

'NOW!' he yelled to Danice. 'Grab the first one you find!'

As Danice jumped into the water, Simon pretended to aim his eel at his foe. But then he suddenly turned and threw it at the front row of prisoners.

There was instant turmoil. Prisoners leapt in all directions.

'Control those prisoners!' the warden yelled.

Simon saw the confusion on his opponent's face and knew his plan had a chance of working.

'Got it! A big one!' Danice shouted.

'Me too!' Simon grabbed hold of another. 'Toss them. As far as you can!'

They heaved the eels with all their strength. One dropped flat onto the head of a guard, making him shriek in agony and stagger into a group of prisoners. The prisoners scattered in terror as the eel thrashed amongst them.

'Stop! Stop there!' the warden bellowed. 'No one moves. *No one!*'

Simon turned to Danice. 'I'm going to grab one more, and then we go!'

There was chaos as the guards tried to corral the prisoners and stop them storming the gates.

Simon pounced onto a final eel. He tossed it into a group of guards who were closing in. They fell over each other in their panic to get away.

'Game over! Let's run!' Simon shouted.

Simon and Danice lumbered through the water to the edge of the pond. They struggled to shed their boots.

'Stop there!' a guard yelled, running around the edge of the pond.

Simon and Danice dashed straight into a mass of rioting prisoners and were immediately swallowed up in the mob. They pushed their way through the crowd and Simon came face to face with the boy he had been fighting.

'Good luck!' Simon grinned.

The boy scowled and took a swing at Simon. But the jostling of the other prisoners quickly separated them, and the boy soon disappeared into the pack.

'Nearly there!' Simon shouted back to Danice.

They pushed hard through the last knot of prisoners and emerged on the open ground beside the hill.

'The fence!' Simon panted. 'Don't forget to activate your springers!'

'Two prisoners are escaping!' the warden roared behind them.

The fence was about six metres high, its top trimmed with sharp shards of wire.

'I'm ready!' Danice shouted.

'One—two—!'

They hit the ground like a drill team, bounded into the air, cleared the fence and broke their landing by tumbling down the sloping bank beyond. For a few seconds, they lay there, puffing to catch their breath.

Simon activated his wrist pilot and retracted his helmet. 'Let's go. The guards'll be after us any minute!'

'Into the forest!' Danice pointed at the wall of redwoods in front of them.

Wet and bedraggled, they got back to their feet and hobbled into the shelter of the trees.

26

'The mission time has now passed forty-eight hours,' Harry reported to the professor and Captain Cutler. 'It's into midmorning of the third day.'

The mood was tense. Cutler and McPhee were silent as they assessed the options. Behind them, Taylor, Ivan and Nick anxiously kept their eyes on the Operations Screen.

'What's the latest on Simon and Danice's position?' Cutler asked.

'Our satellite's just returned over the area,' Harry replied. 'They're in the forest now, near that agricultural land we identified earlier.'

The two red dots flashed on the screen.

'Stationary?'

'Hard to tell, sir. Stationary, then some movement, then stationary again. That's been the pattern.'

Cutler frowned with concentration. 'How far are

they from our original timeline? The point to which they had to return for pick-up?'

'About thirty k's,' Harry replied.

'Difficult terrain?'

'Could be, sir. Forests and rocky gorges, from what we can work out.'

'Anything to stop us sending in a new timeline and picking them up?' McPhee asked.

'No, sir.'

'Could I advise against that, Professor?' Cutler interrupted.

'We have two temponauts a long way from their intended zone of operation. And they're way overdue,' McPhee said. 'Your reasons for not sending a new timeline?'

'My reason is the mission,' Cutler said bluntly. 'We need to give them a chance to get the information we need. From our monitoring so far, they've not reached the Chieftain's fortress. That is our principal objective. We should give them extra time to complete their mission.'

'And what if they're in real danger?' McPhee asked.

'We've no evidence of that yet.' Cutler's eyes flicked to the screen and then back to the professor. 'Yes, they're way off course, and yes, the mission's gone forty-eight hours. But there might be a good reason for that. We look for initiative from our temponauts. I say we give them a chance to show it.'

McPhee looked thoughtful. 'Very well, your assessment is valid. But we'll activate our emergency response mode, all the same.'

Cutler turned to Ivan, Taylor and Nick. 'I suggest the three of you suit up. We may need you for a rescue operation at short notice.'

'Sir! Yes, sir!' the three temponauts replied.

'Keep down!' Simon dragged Danice from the track into the cover of a thick patch of chest-high ferns. They had discarded their tattered overalls to let their time-travel suits provide automatic camouflage. But there was no point taking risks.

There was a pounding of hoofs and a mounted guard urged his horse along the path and past them. He galloped on into the forest, scattering a flight of small grey birds.

There were shouts from more guards in the distance.

'We have to keep moving,' Simon said. 'How far away is the Chieftain's fortress?'

'Thirty k's to the north,' Danice replied. 'It could take us a couple of days to get there.'

'That's too long!' Simon muttered. More hoof beats approached along the track. There was a flash of a horse and rider coming through the trees towards them.

Simon leapt to his feet. 'I've got an idea!' he said.

'What are you doing?' Danice hissed.

'Stay down and wait here!' Simon said. He grabbed a broken branch about two metres long and scurried to the edge of the track. To his right there was a metre-high slab of rock. He ran to it and crouched behind, out of sight, timing his next move.

The beating hoofs drew closer. Just as they reached a crescendo, Simon leapt onto the rock.

'*Yaaaaa!*' he shouted.

He swung the branch and thumped the rider a powerful blow on the chest.

The man's face froze in shock and he fainted. Then he slid off the still-moving horse and toppled soundlessly into the long grass at the side of the trail. His arms and legs twitched slightly.

'Let's get out of here before he recovers,' Simon said, jumping down from the rock.

Danice had chased after the horse, and already held the reins of the dun mare in her hands. 'Easy, whoa there!' she said. Then she turned to Simon. 'You can ride, can't you?'

'A bit. How about you?'

'No.'

The horse whinnied and skittered a few flighty steps sideways.

'There, girl, easy now, easy,' Simon said softly, taking the reins and stroking the mare's neck.

The horse snorted and swished her tail.

'Good girl,' Simon said, and in a flash he was

up on her back. 'Now we can get back to our next objective,' he grinned. 'Check out the Chieftain's place!'

He held out his hand and helped Danice climb up behind him.

Danice placed a hand on Simon's shoulder. 'I'm not sure the Chieftain's fortress is such a great idea. Perhaps we should call the mission off. We should get back to the pick-up point and wait until they send back the TPS. That's correct procedure, and I want to do things by the book. If we go AWOL, the Bureau might change their minds about helping my family.'

Simon turned in the saddle. Danice had got it all wrong. He was sure that if they failed to meet all their objectives, their mission status would be downgraded. They would be removed from priority assignments. He couldn't let that happen. 'You've got to be kidding. The mission isn't finished yet!'

He flicked the reins, the mare sniffed the wind and they galloped off.

The face in the mirror was that of an old man. Deep wrinkles furrowed the Chieftain's brow, and brown liver spots freckled his cheeks, chin and neck. For a few moments, he stared sadly at the image of a man who looked so much older than his actual calendar years.

'You're not the man you used to be, old boy,' he said, allowing himself a rare sigh.

There was a knock on the door.

'Yes? Enter!'

O'Bray opened the door and peered in.

'O'Bray! Good, I wanted to see you.'

'Yes, boss?'

'That report, earlier,' the Chieftain said. 'Those two time travellers. Any news?'

'Yes, a little,' O'Bray replied. 'Our informants tell me they've escaped from the Prison Farms.'

The Chieftain raised his eyebrows with interest. 'And where are they now?'

'No idea, boss. But I've sent our airship and some guards to take a look out there.'

'All right, I'll leave that in your hands.'

'And, boss, I've put the Time Accelerator on standby as you requested,' O'Bray said. 'Should I program some specific coordinates for your destination?'

'No. I'll take care of that,' said the Chieftain. He gave a mysterious smile. 'We go wherever we want, O'Bray. The whole of history is out there, ready and waiting for us.'

27

The mare was soon in full stride and, although she was carrying both Danice and Simon, she made good time as they galloped along the margins of the forest.

Within half an hour, they were amongst rugged, timbered hills. Simon slowed the pace as the track turned into the forest and began to snake through gullies.

'It's a bit rough through here,' Simon observed. 'Is this the right way?'

'Yes,' Danice replied. Then, after a moment, she said, 'Simon, the more I think about it, the more I reckon we should end this mission. They'll be going into emergency mode. We should be, too!'

'And?'

'They'll send the satellite back. At eight-hour intervals.' She tugged his arm. 'You read your manual, didn't you?'

'Yeah, I read it! I know the procedure.'

'Then let's abort the mission,' Danice pleaded. 'Let's get back to the pick-up location and wait. It's the safest option.'

'This isn't about safety,' Simon snapped. 'We've got a job to do. What about our mission?'

Danice shrugged. 'We tried. They'll understand.'

The mare splashed through a creek, sending sprays of water over the riders. Simon wiped his eyes and face, using this as an excuse not to respond. He kept silent as they plunged into a broader gorge, going deeper and deeper into the forest.

Simon considered their options. Danice was partly right. As a result of having been captured, they were way behind schedule, and they were still a long way from their final and most important objective. He also had no doubt that Mission Control was at this very moment planning their extraction from this timezone. Yet he didn't want to admit defeat. They had come too far in time and space to give up now.

'Look,' Simon said at last, 'I'm going to finish this mission.' He twisted in the saddle to look back at Danice. 'We get into the Chieftain's place, we find out what we can about him. And *then* we return. That's how I want to do it.'

'It's too risky!' Danice cried. 'Unless we go back to the TPS location, the Bureau can't find us.'

The mare suddenly stopped. The track ahead was broken by a chasm fifteen metres wide and at least fifty metres deep. A sapling bridge had been built to cross the gap. It was a primitive construction of a dozen logs with their ends buried in the dirt on each side of the chasm.

Danice peered around Simon's shoulder. 'Hey, does that look safe?'

The mare nickered nervously and pawed the ground.

'I'd better lead her across,' Simon said.

He helped Danice dismount before swinging out of the saddle himself. 'You get to the other side,' he said.

Danice took a few steps onto the bridge. The greying timbers had been partly flattened on top after years of weathering and constant use.

'Watch this one!' she said, pointing to a log that had split in the middle and sagged below the level of the others. 'It looks shaky!'

'I see it,' Simon replied. He started to lead the mare across. She stepped uncertainly, blowing through her nostrils.

'Easy, girl, easy,' Simon said soothingly.

The mare took one step, then another, before gathering confidence and clopping delicately across the bridge.

On the other side of the chasm, the track split in two.

'We have to decide here,' Danice said. 'The track to the left goes up that hill, climbs pretty high, then goes down in the direction of the Fire Caves. We could see my family there, then get back to our pick-up point. The other one goes more or less straight to the Chieftain's place.'

'What do you want to do?' Simon asked.

'You know what I think.'

'Okay, you go and see your family, and decide what you want to do from there.' Simon mounted the horse and gathered up the reins. 'And I'll keep going to the Chieftain's fortress.'

'But you don't even know the area!'

'I'll work it out,' Simon said. 'With or without you.'

'You're too stubborn!' Danice groaned.

Simon said nothing.

Danice stared along one track, then the other.

'Now what is it?' Simon asked.

In the distance, somewhere close and to the north of them, Danice heard a pulsating sound, like an engine. 'Can you hear that?' she asked.

'No. What?' Simon said.

Danice listened again. A few birds called out in the surrounding trees. But now the other sound was gone. 'It's nothing,' she said. 'I just thought I heard something, you know, like airship engines.'

'I didn't hear a thing.'

Danice shrugged. Then she looked again at the two tracks, and back at Simon. 'All right, you win,' she said at last. 'We go on with the mission.'

'Are you sure?'

Danice kept her doubts to herself. 'Yes,' she said.

Simon smiled. 'Hey, we won't get eaten by wild beasts on the way, will we?'

'So long as we don't stand around gossiping.'

Simon reached down and helped Danice climb up behind him.

Then he turned the horse's head along the right-hand track.

Half a kilometre on, they emerged from the gorge into a narrow, grassy valley.

Suddenly Danice gasped, 'Simon! Watch out!'

A score of armed men ran out of the cover of the trees and quickly encircled them. They pointed guns at Simon and Danice's heads.

Danice clung to Simon as the mare snorted and wheeled.

'Who are they? Prison guards?' Simon asked.

'I don't know who they are,' Danice replied. 'They're wearing civilian clothes!'

'Try to escape, and we shoot!' a man in a peaked cap shouted. He stepped forward and grabbed the mare's reins. 'You're coming with us!' he said.

An airship suddenly slid into view overhead and loomed above them. Its shadow darkened the clearing.

The sun set in the west, and columns of smoke drifted over Old City. Sirens and shouting filled the streets. Damien and Bigdad hurried down one of the lanes that led away from the plaza, heading towards the north of the city.

'So far, so good,' Bigdad said. 'The airship tower will be under minimum guard by now. All units will have been sent to quell the riots.'

'Our comrades did well to find so much fuel for the fires,' Damien said. 'I didn't think there was that much firewood in the city!'

'We've been stockpiling it for a while.' Bigdad grinned. 'But I didn't expect every low-life crim from the slums would join in the riot as well.'

'Even if they don't have a clue what it's all about.'

'It doesn't matter. Anyone who joins in helps our cause,' Bigdad said. As they reached the corner, he hesitated. 'The airship tower is down the end of the next street. Four of my men are meeting us there.'

Damien gulped. It made no difference that he had travelled into the past, he still felt nervous and excited at the prospect of action against the Tribunes. 'What's the plan?'

'Once we've secured the tower,' Bigdad said, 'you should get back to your mother and Alli, and the other folk. Tell them to prepare for the journey to the Far Lands. But we won't get to you until after first light tomorrow.'

'Why that long?' Damien asked.

'We can't navigate the ship very far at night. It's too dangerous,' Bigdad replied. 'There's a clearing in the forest, just north-west of the city. We'll take the captured airship there and keep it out of sight, below the level of the trees, till just before dawn. Then we'll come to the Fire Caves.'

'We'll be ready,' Damien said. 'But what about Danice? We haven't heard from her!'

Bigdad's face softened. 'She's busy doing what she came back to do. In the meantime, let's steal this airship!'

Damien nodded, although he wished he had his father's confidence in his sister and her friend.

28

1 don't like this,' Danice said. 'I don't even know who these people are. Where are they taking us? I hope we're not going back to that prison.'

She huddled next to Simon on the floor of the airship cabin.

Simon glanced at the two men opposite them. They chatted quietly and occasionally laughed. 'I can't work it out, either,' he said. 'Are they prison guards?'

'They're not wearing uniforms,' Danice replied, 'but they've got guns and side-arms, which the prison guards don't carry. Maybe they're Special Forces. From the Tribunes.'

Simon lifted his eyes to the cabin window. All he could see was the sky. 'I've been trying to follow which direction we've been taking. When we left the valley back there, I'm sure they turned the airship around. Wouldn't that mean we're heading *away* from the prison? In the same direction we were riding before they captured us?'

Danice thought a moment. 'Yeah, I think you're right.' She glanced out the window above them, and at the sky beyond. 'And if you look at those clouds, they have shadows on the right side, and the pink of the sunset on the left.'

Simon nodded. 'Which means the sun is to the left, which means the west is to the left.'

'And if we turned around, that means you're right,' she said. 'We must be heading north, towards the city. Away from the prison.'

Simon glanced again at the men who were guarding them, then suddenly jumped to his feet and looked out of the window.

One of the men growled, 'Get down! Stay where you are!'

Simon sank obediently back to the floor.

'What did you see?' Danice whispered.

'A big clump of trees, probably the forest, and maybe some cliffs to our left.'

There was a shudder as the airship altered course. The full power of the propeller engines diminished to a throbbing pulse as they began to lose altitude.

'I reckon this means we're coming in to dock,' Simon said.

Danice gulped. 'But whose dock? And where? And what are they going to do with us this time?'

'The satellite is passing over Old City again,' Harry reported.

'Have we got vision?' Professor McPhee asked.

'Night's falling, sir, we're on infrared,' Harry replied, bringing up the stream from the satellite.

The city plaza and the nearby streets came up on a smaller viewing screen. A series of white, bright patches flared on and off in different locations.

'What are we seeing?' McPhee asked.

'There appear to be a lot of small fires in the central city and some of the nearby housing areas,' Harry said. 'And vision a short while ago showed a number of vehicles, and possibly crowds of people, moving through the city. The crowds were growing in size, then breaking into smaller groups, then growing again in size. A bit chaotic.'

'Some sort of civil unrest?' Cutler asked.

'That's a strong possibility. Vision's not top quality, sir. And we have no close images.'

McPhee frowned. 'What about Simon and Danice?'

Harry switched the vision to two red dots. 'They've moved a considerable distance since we last tracked them. They've moved over twenty kilometres in a fairly short time.'

'Didn't we assume they were on foot last time, going through pretty rough country?' Cutler said.

'Yes, sir. My guess is they've now taken some form of transport.'

'A high-speed vehicle?'

'Impossible to say,' Harry replied. 'This vision was recorded two minutes ago, to the south of the city. We can see the two red dots. But we can't see by what means they got there.'

'So for some reason, they've not returned to the TPS pick-up point out in the Big Forest,' McPhee said.

'Perhaps they're trying to complete their mission,' Cutler suggested.

'That could be so,' McPhee replied. 'But it's time to extract them. Their inexperience might be showing here. They've clearly not stuck to the mission plan, for whatever reason. They've also overstayed their allotted time, and it's far too costly for us to keep this operation going indefinitely. I want personnel sent to provide on-ground assistance. Are our other temponauts kitted up?'

'Yes, they're ready,' Cutler said.

'Activate a timeline to the south of the city. To the exact time and last recorded location for Simon and Danice.' McPhee concentrated on the screen. 'Full power and Priority Red!'

Simon flapped a hand in front of his nose. '*Whew!* This smoke! Are all these blazing torches and the gold-toothed skulls for real? It looks like the set for a B-grade movie.'

'I've been here before,' Danice said as they were

led through the front entrance of a cave by a pair of guards. 'This is the Chieftain's place.'

'So, we made it!' Simon whispered. 'We finally get to meet this dude.'

A look of distaste passed over Danice's face. 'Don't get too carried away,' she said. 'Everyone I know hates him.'

A man's voice came from deep in the shadows of the cave. 'Come!' he said.

'Move forward! Bow to the Chieftain!' a guard said, pushing Simon and Danice from behind.

As his eyes adjusted to the gloom, Simon saw a white-robed figure sitting on a red granite throne.

O'Bray appeared at their side and glared at them. 'Show respect before the Chieftain,' he said.

Danice lowered her head respectfully, but Simon found it hard to take the situation seriously. The cave, the skulls and the eerie lighting seemed like a theatrical show. Perhaps it scared the local people into submission, but to Simon it seemed silly.

He squinted through the clouds of oily smoke, trying to get a better look at the Chieftain. But the hood of the Chieftain's robe covered his face, leaving only a firm jaw and lips visible beneath. Tattoos decorated his bare arms up to the elbow.

'Danice, I'm surprised to see you with this stranger,' the Chieftain said. 'And in such an elaborate outfit. It's a time-travel suit, isn't it?'

'Yes, it is, Chieftain,' Danice mumbled nervously.

'Someone's been lying to me!' the Chieftain said. 'The last I heard was that you had gone missing. Yet here you are! Tell me what really happened.'

Danice glanced at Simon and he shook his head. She remained silent.

'Your silence confirms my suspicions,' the Chieftain said. He raised a hand. 'O'Bray, leave the boy here with me. Take Danice away. But I don't want her hurt or mistreated, understand?'

'Yes, boss, I understand.'

O'Bray took Danice's arm and led her off to an inner room.

Simon squinted into the gloom where the Chieftain sat.

'Some of your conversations have been reported to me,' the Chieftain said. 'You seem to be curious about my men. I will admit, I made them dress like civilians, just in case anyone saw them while they were out there picking you up. I like to keep my activities as covert as possible. Normally, my guards wear camouflage uniforms.'

Simon nodded and waited for the Chieftain to go on. A small smile seemed to hover on the man's lips.

'So,' the Chieftain said at last. 'I didn't think I'd be found so soon.'

'Sorry, but I didn't find you,' Simon replied. 'You . . . um . . . found us. And brought us here.'

'Why did they send you?'

'Who do you mean?'

'The Time Bureau,' the Chieftain said. 'I suspected they'd get onto my trail eventually.' He paused again. 'But I didn't think they'd send you, of all people.'

Simon didn't know what to think. How much did this guy know, he wondered. Was this some kind of guessing game?

The Chieftain didn't wait for an answer. He rose from the throne and came slowly down the steps to the floor of the cave until he was in the full glare of the torchlight. Then he reached up and drew back his hood to reveal long, white hair and a tanned, wrinkled face.

Simon found himself staring into bright blue eyes that twinkled with humour. He felt a lump in his chest, but didn't know why.

'Who are you?' he asked. 'What is this place all about?'

'I collect gold-plated skulls,' the Chieftain grinned. *'You've got to have a hobby.'*

Simon gulped. That familiar phrase spoken with that familiar accent. He stared open-mouthed at this old man with his heavily lined face and white hair. 'Dad! Is . . . is that you?'

'Hi, Simon! Welcome to my lair.'

Hale Savage reached out both his hands. Simon ran forward and let his father's arms encircle him.

'Dad!' He felt like a small child again. 'Dad!'

'Good to see you, son,' Hale said. 'You don't know how good it is to see you.'

29

Half an hour later, Simon and his father were in a comfortable living room, several chambers away from the theatrical setting of the Chieftain's cave. Simon was sitting on a leather couch by an open fire. There were bookshelves on both sides of the fireplace. On the opposite wall were more shelves, and dozens of thin, corked glass jars full of multi-coloured seeds.

We could be at home in Bondi, Simon thought, except that he was with a man greatly changed in both appearance and manner—tattooed and white-haired. And older and frailer from the stresses of time travel.

'I don't get it, Dad,' Simon said. 'Why did you leave us?'

A flicker of guilt passed over his father's face. 'You've no idea how sorry I was to leave you behind.'

'Sorry!' Simon replied. 'That's pathetic. Mum was

devastated. She didn't know what to do with herself. Lil couldn't eat or sleep . . . and . . . do you know how bad it is to . . . to lose someone?' Simon paused. 'We missed you.'

'It wasn't a one-way street,' Hale said. 'I missed you, too.'

'But you tricked us. We thought you were dead! How could you do that?'

'I had to do it.' For a second, there was a hint of fear in Hale's eyes. 'For various reasons I hope you'll understand one day. I had to get away. From . . . from many things.'

'Then why didn't you take us with you?' Simon asked.

'I had planned to do that.' Hale picked up an iron poker, leaned forward and stirred a pile of glowing coals in the fireplace. 'But things happened too quickly. Things that I didn't like.'

'Things that were more important than us?'

'Yes,' Hale replied. 'At the time they were. Yes.'

Simon looked at his father with new eyes. Hale had dropped the whole Chieftain act and left it behind in the other room. But what sort of man had he become? Who was he really?

'While we're asking questions, I have one or two for you,' Hale said, breaking another coal with the poker. 'There are a few things I need to know.'

Simon shrugged. 'Well, you're not the only one who wants answers.'

'How did they recruit you . . . the Time Bureau?'

Simon considered his answer for a few moments.

'Divided loyalties?' Hale asked.

'Maybe.'

'Okay, here's something *you* need to know. I know more about that Time Bureau than anyone alive. Ask me anything about its operations, and I'll be able to tell you. So, how did they recruit you?'

'They came to the house,' Simon said. 'They did a genetic scanning with some gadget. Then they offered me a place at Mayfield Manor.'

'Ah, yes, genetic time searches, as the professor calls them. Finding young people ideal for time travel. Well, *that* wasn't my idea. The professor was always keen to get new recruits.' He turned sadly from the fire to look at Simon. 'Obviously, it's working.'

'There's a few of us temponauts now.'

'Ah, yes. And am I right in guessing that Danice is one of them? That was a clever trick by the Bureau. Abducting her so that she could bring you to me.'

'I suppose,' Simon said, not sure how to interpret his father's tone.

'Don't worry, son, I'm not angry with you! But tell me, did they test Lil?'

'I guess so. But she's at some smart school now, so I figure they didn't want to recruit her. Anyway, you know she's only just turned eleven.'

Simon saw a glimmer of relief pass over his father's

face, but he quickly controlled it and stared back into the flames. 'Here is a more important question: before they sent you here, did they say anything in particular about me?'

'Not much.'

'Well?'

'Just that you'd invented time travel. That you'd been working under a lot of pressure,' Simon said. 'I think they were worried that you had run off with a lot of research, or a lot of knowledge you hadn't shared about time travel.'

Hale smiled. 'How right they were about that!'

Simon jumped up. 'Dad, come back with me! You can live with Mum and Lil in Bristol.'

'Son, I'm not going back. I'm . . .' Hale stopped himself. 'Well, if I go anywhere, I'll choose where I go for myself.'

'What about Mum? And Lil and me!'

'I'm sorry.'

'I don't get it!' Simon protested. 'That's what I don't understand. The fake suicide, and all that!'

'You really want to hear?' Hale asked. 'If you do, sit down and I'll tell you.'

Simon sank back into the soft leather.

Hale turned away from the fire and stood with his back to the hearth. 'Simon, I spent the best part of ten years developing time travel. I came across the basic principles when I was working on something else: black holes and time loops. I'll cut a very long story short.' Hale started pacing the floor. 'Basically, within a few years we had a working Time Accelerator. And I had proved that it worked. I thought I should be the one to test it out. I ended up doing more trips than I should have.' He pushed a lock of long white hair off his forehead. 'The truth is, my body's wearing out. As you can see, it's ageing quickly. I've been in and out of the Spin Box too many times. It wrecks you, even when you're only in your forties.'

Simon nodded. The evidence was in front of him. His father looked closer to seventy.

'Once we had a Time Accelerator, things started to change in the Bureau. You see, I invented time travel for peaceful purposes.' Hale's eyes flicked to the jars of seeds along the wall. 'I did it for research, to acquire knowledge, to understand the universe. That was my sole aim.' His tone changed and became harder, sharper. 'But some people in the military tried to get hold of it, in order to control the system directly. Their aim was to use it as a weapon.'

'Do you mean Professor McPhee and Captain Cutler?'

'No, not them,' Hale said. 'They're basically good men. A few far-sighted politicians have managed to put the Time Bureau in their hands.' Hale shrugged. 'But for how long this will last, I don't know.'

He stopped by the couch and rested his hand on Simon's head. 'Son, I know so much more about time travel than they will ever know.' His eyes glinted. 'Its power, its reach across the vast gaps of time. You and your temponaut friends have only just scratched the surface.'

He sat down beside Simon and went silent.

'Dad, are you okay?'

Hale nodded. 'Simon, you know how I said I had to get away?'

'Yeah. Was it those military guys?'

'It happened at a meeting in Sydney, with international defence personnel. I hinted at my research into moving people across time. Not one, two, or three individuals like you are doing now. But scores, maybe hundreds of people at a time. It was foolish, no, stupid of me to mention it to them. But I was trying to get extra funding for the Bureau. To pay for some other research and development.'

Simon concentrated with every cell of his brain.

'Some of the military people saw the possibilities of moving platoons and companies of soldiers through time,' Hale went on. 'This would give them incredible strategic advantages in battle, and in guerrilla warfare. In fact, in any conflict.'

'But that's interfering with history!' Simon said. 'They're always going on about how we're not supposed to interfere.'

'Time travel is interfering with history by its very nature,' Hale replied. 'The Bureau tries to keep to rules, as we all do. But they sent you here, to the future, didn't they? To investigate and stop the mysterious Chieftain and his gold-hunting expeditions! How is that *not* interfering with history?'

Simon shrugged. 'I don't know. It's too complicated for me!'

'I knew they'd get onto me, once they perfected the Timeline Monitoring System,' Hale said. 'Son, time travel is infinite in its possibilities and, once it's mastered, there are no longer any rules. That's what I learnt from those military people. For them, time is a weapon. And I wasn't going to give them this weapon. But they demanded all my research data . . . and they wanted it straightaway.'

'So what happened?' Simon asked.

'It all came to a head the day before I disappeared from that beach,' Hale continued. 'These guys contacted me at work and started threatening me. They accused me of holding back information so I could sell it to other governments and to other military powers. They accused me of treason, and worse. They said they'd lock me up and throw away the key unless I handed my research over.'

'That's crazy!'

'They certainly didn't think so! I had all the data. The only problem was, I'd hidden it some time earlier.' He waved his arm to indicate the Chieftain's fortress. 'I'd hidden it here, actually, on one of my trips to this timezone.'

'One of those times when you were away,' Simon

said. 'We thought they were business trips. But they were time-trips!'

Hale nodded. 'I set up this place as a refuge in case I ever needed it. It was my natural caution, I suppose. It seemed remote, out of sight from a twenty-first century point of view.'

'So what did the military guys do?'

'They pressured me hard, but I still refused to release my research. Early the next morning, I got a tip-off that they were sniffing around the Time Bureau asking for my home address. I knew this was serious. I ran like a scared rabbit. And I'm sorry. It wasn't fair on Mum and Lil. Or on you.'

'You broke our hearts.' It didn't feel great saying it, but Simon was glad he had.

Hale flinched and looked back at the fire.

'I'm . . . I'm sorry, Dad,' Simon said.

'No, it's all right. I know what I did. I've had to live with it.'

Simon tried a more conciliatory tone. 'So, how did you manage to get away?'

'It was easier than I thought, really,' Hale replied. 'That morning, I managed to get back to the laboratory building in Sydney. I had time to program a TPS at the Time Accelerator there to materialise at a particular time at a particular beach.' Hale got up and went to the bookshelf and took down a small black box with a keyboard and press-button controls. 'Then I got in my car and drove down there. I used this Zone Relocator to remotely operate the TPS and to get me here to the twenty-fourth century.' He smiled. 'Another one of my inventions they're still to cotton onto at the Bureau.'

Simon showed his wrist pilot. 'They've got Zone Activators.'

'But this is the next advance in that technology,' Hale said. 'It's like a homing device. You don't have to get back to the location where the TPS is going to appear . . . you can move the timeline to where you are in the field.'

'So each temponaut has control of the TPS,' Simon said. 'You program a new location, maybe a new pick-up point, whenever you want it. That'd be handy.'

'I'm impressed with your grasp of the technology,' Hale said.

He picked up the skull of a tiny marsupial from the coffee table. 'Anyway, this is the place I escaped to.' He laughed. 'I had to make myself look fiercer and more powerful than anyone else. I needed gold to buy my way into everyone's good books. It's real survival of the fittest in this century.'

'I know, I've experienced some of it,' Simon said. 'But, Dad, did the Time Bureau know you were the Chieftain?' he asked. 'Did they know you were here?'

'Perhaps they suspected it. Time travel is a rare technology and owned only by very few.'

'It's just that I found out they red-flagged the

timeline from Kiama Beach,' Simon said. 'They must have known where it went and didn't want anyone else to find out.'

Hale nodded. 'You might be right. And they sent you to find me. Was that a coincidence, do you think?'

Simon didn't know what to say. Had Cutler and McPhee deliberately recruited him for the Time Bureau, in order to use him for this mission? It seemed more than likely. Or had they had some other reason?

'Simon, I don't expect you to be able to answer that. These are questions for other people to answer.' He shook his head and smiled. 'Anyway, I want you to know I haven't been wasting my time here. Come . . . there's something downstairs that I want you to see. Catch!'

Simon grabbed the skull that his father tossed to him. He hurriedly put it on the table, and followed Hale into the next room. So many questions were rolling around in his mind. But, for now, he found it best not to think at all.

Damien kicked aside the wrecked remains of a pushcart and jumped over a mess of broken glass. A group of rioters ran down the middle of the lane, shouting wildly, their arms full of clothes, food and other looted goods.

He stood back to let them pass. These people

were not from the Underground. More than likely they didn't have anything to do with the real cause of the unrest. They were just people taking the opportunity to grab a few of the things they needed. Keen to avoid meeting any more of them, Damien darted around the next corner and glimpsed the city wall beyond the lane's end.

There were only fifty metres left before the end of the lane and the embankment that led down to the tunnel. He paused in the last of the shadows and peered into the open. Then he pulled his head back as a troop of soldiers marched by on their way to their next riot-control job in the city.

As Damien waited for a chance to safely cross the open ground, he glanced up at the red glow in the sky. The flames were now engulfing some of the dwellings on the far side of town, near the air tower that Bigdad had just captured and where they had successfully taken control of the airship.

But now, doubts flooded Damien's mind. Should he go with his family to the Far Lands? Was that their best chance of survival? Or should he stay? He suddenly felt unsure as to whether he wanted to leave the Chieftain and the work that had kept them fed all the long months since Bigdad was taken to the city. The time-travel work was exciting. And maybe there was a better chance of survival to be found in exploring other times than there was in escaping to the Far Lands.

Damien eventually shook his head. The way ahead was finally clear. There was no point wondering about time travel. His duty was to make sure Mama and Alli were safe, and that meant preparing them for their journey. After that, there might be time to think about his future.

Damien dashed across the open ground and down the embankment. He opened the waste tunnel's metal grille, checked that no one had seen him, and crawled inside.

30

The old electric elevator clanked deeper and deeper into the ground. Through the gaps in the steel-mesh cage, Simon watched the sedimentary layers of rock pass—yellow, orange, clay red, brown and even a few flashes of brighter crystalline colour. After what seemed like forever, the elevator lurched to a halt and Hale opened the door and stepped out.

'*Phew*, it's freezing!' Simon said. 'I thought it was always hotter underground!' He followed his father into a long, dark tunnel carved into the solid rock. 'Is this where your Spin Box is located?'

'No, we passed that level on our way down.' Hale flicked a switch and a sequence of lights flickered on.

'I get it,' Simon replied. 'This is where you keep your gold.'

'Some of it, yes, but that's not the real purpose of this place,' Hale said. 'The gold has only been a means to an end, believe me.'

Their footsteps echoed loudly in the cold tunnel as they walked towards a thick steel door at the end of the rocky passage. Lumps of broken rock were scattered over the ground and Simon kicked a chunk out of his path.

'Dad, is this area safe?' he asked. 'The place is falling apart.'

'Just bits of the tunnel wall coming loose,' Hale said. 'Lots of these underground walls were rendered in a mixture of rocks and concrete. They've been repaired over the years, but they're wearing away. I do what I can, but maintenance is expensive.'

They reached the steel door and Simon watched as his father punched some numbers into a code lock. With a heavy grinding sound, the door slowly rumbled on rails into a recess in the side of the tunnel. Simon's father stepped inside and Simon followed.

Beyond the door was a huge rectangular room with a concrete floor and walls, measuring about fifty by thirty metres. A dozen rows of floor-to-ceiling steel shelves stretched down the length of the space.

'This was once a storage room for a Particle Accelerator built about a century ago, just after they constructed the power station,' Hale said. 'I was able to get the Accelerator working again and to build my own Spin Box, but I decided to use this room for something else,' he continued, grabbing a thick overcoat from a hook beside the door.

'Why's it s-so cold?' Simon asked. His travel suit

was adjusting his body warmth, but he still felt the icy air on his face.

'I've had it refrigerated to four degrees below zero. It's the ideal temperature to keep things safe and preserved,' Hale replied.

'Keep what safe and preserved?'

Hale crossed to a row of shelves and lifted the lid from one of hundreds of large, solid plastic containers.

'Those are eskies!' Simon exclaimed. 'Where did you get so many of them?'

Hale grinned. 'I got a factory up in the city to copy one I brought with me. They're not nearly as good as the ones you get in twenty-first century Australia, but they serve their purpose.'

Hale reached inside. There was a tinkle of glass against glass. 'Here, this is what I'm keeping safe.'

He held up a sealed glass storage-jar filled with thousands of tiny, dark seeds.

Simon looked around the vast room. The fact that his father had gone on collecting seeds was not surprising. What made it staggering was the sheer size of his efforts. 'Dad, are you telling me this whole place is filled with seeds?'

Hale spread his arms to encompass all corners of the room. 'This is my World Seed Bank. Millions of seeds, tens of thousands of different species. The seeds of trees, of hundreds of grains, of a myriad fruits and vegetables.'

He took out several more jars from a selection of eskies. 'Thousands of species of plants have disappeared in the last three centuries, during the wars, as well as from Earth warming up.' He shook one jar of light-brown grains. 'This is a strain of wheat, a high-productivity grain that has long been extinct.'

'Then where did you find it?'

'I made quite a few expeditions back in time myself.' Hale ran his fingers across the wrinkled skin of his face. 'It's taken its toll on me, as you can see. But it was worth it. I found a lot of this collection in just a few trips to a Seed Bank in northern Norway. It had been sealed up in the twenty-second century . . . and left for me to find!'

Hale produced another jar of tiny seeds. 'These will grow high-yield carrots.'

'I hate carrots.'

'So I recall.' Hale put the jars back in their places. 'It took me a while to learn of the devastation to agriculture and food production in this world as it exists now.' He shrugged. 'I couldn't do much to help people of my own time. So these seeds are my gift to the twenty-fourth century. They might help Earth's population as it starts to re-establish itself.'

Simon lifted his eyebrows and smiled. 'Interfering with history . . . again.'

'It doesn't matter how we try to disguise it,' Hale replied, 'we are always changing things when we time travel. It comes with the job. You'll learn that as you travel more across the centuries.'

'Maybe I will, maybe I won't,' Simon said. 'I found you, Dad. I guess that's all I really wanted to do. Maybe I won't want to stay with the Time Bureau after this.'

'There's a very good reason for you to stay,' Hale said. 'Mainly because your mum and Lil——'

A loud buzz suddenly interrupted him, and Simon was left wondering what his father had been about to tell him.

'Hold on,' Hale said, picking up the receiver from a wall phone. 'Hello . . . Yes, O'Bray . . .' As Hale listened, his face changed quickly from interest to concern. 'Very well. Put the Spin Box on standby. Yes, make all preparations.' Hale hung up. 'We have to return to the surface. The Tribunes are making trouble!'

'What sort of trouble? Where?'

'Big trouble, right here. They want my gold, I guess.' Hale took off his coat and threw it aside. 'I've been expecting this. Those men have just been biding their time.'

'We have to get back to Danice!' Simon said.

'We'll look after her. She's in safe hands.'

Simon followed his father into the passage-way and watched as he activated the code lock outside.

'My Seed Bank will have to stay sealed up for a

while longer,' Hale said. 'For a better day! Earth will revive, Simon.'

The thick steel door slowly rumbled out from its recess in the rock. Within a few seconds, it had slammed shut, sealing the seed room tight again.

'Come on!' Hale said.

They hurried back towards the elevator.

'Dad, why did you order the activation of the Spin Box?'

Hale didn't answer.

Simon silently followed his father along the tunnel. He had a bad feeling about what might happen next.

31

The ground rumbled underfoot as another explosion from outside rocked the Chieftain's fortress.

O'Bray hurried across to Hale as he and Simon left the elevator and entered the main cave. 'They're attacking us outside the northern gate,' he said. 'And they're coming from the west, up the cliffs from the forest! We can't fight them off on two sides!'

Simon turned to his father. 'Is all this just to get your gold, Dad?'

O'Bray stared in astonishment. 'He's . . . your son?' He blinked, then quickly recovered. 'Boss, the Tribunes think you're behind all the trouble in the city and the riot out at the Prison Farms.'

Simon felt a tinge of guilt. He was responsible for the prison riot. And partly responsible for the city riots, too.

'The Tribunes arrested some of the rioters in the city. Three of them were those guards we recently fired for being troublemakers. The Tribunes think the guards are still working for you and that you've incited them to revolt,' O'Bray said. 'They think you're making some sort of grab for power.'

'And who would have given them that impression, eh, O'Bray?' Hale asked.

O'Bray shrugged. 'Who knows?'

'Then tell me, how do you know the cause of these things so soon after they've occurred?'

'The riots in the city and at the Farms have been going all day, boss.'

Hale gave him a steely glare. 'Who, amongst all your informants, had time to come and give you this information, and yet wasn't able to give us warning about an attack from the Tribunes?'

O'Bray avoided meeting Hale's gaze. 'I don't know. But we don't have enough men to hold out against so many. The situation is serious——'

Another explosion trembled through the walls. The skull of a sabre-toothed tiger wobbled and fell with a crash.

O'Bray twitched nervously. 'I've also heard that some slaves have stolen an airship in the city.'

Simon was pleased to hear the news, but kept his thoughts private.

'Good on them,' Hale said. 'I wish them luck.' He took a long look around the cave. 'Well, the Tribunes can take what they want. I'm not staying around to fight. O'Bray, I'll leave the troubles outside to you. Continue the fight, surrender, do whatever you please. Meanwhile, it's time to implement my emergency exit strategy.'

Simon couldn't quite believe what he was hearing. 'Dad?' he asked.

His father ignored him.

'The Accelerator is powering up and will be ready shortly,' O'Bray said.

'And I'll take my reserve supply of gold with me.'

'Yes, boss.'

'Dad, where are you going?' Simon asked with sudden panic. It had only just sunk in that his father wasn't organising resistance to the Tribunes: he was getting ready to leave.

'Simon! Simon!' Danice's voice suddenly echoed through the cave.

More shells exploded outside.

Danice stood in the doorway to the next chamber.

'And yes, there's the question of the girl!' O'Bray said.

'She's free to go home,' Hale replied. 'Or wherever she wants to go. Get things organised for me.'

O'Bray nodded. 'Yes, boss, right away.' He brushed past Danice and headed towards the elevator.

Hale gave a half smile. 'He'll be glad to see me go. He's been keen to get his hands on my riches for a long while.'

Danice stood silently, wary about entering the Chieftain's cave uninvited.

'Danice! It's all right, come in,' Simon said.

She came forward and bowed from habit. She tried to hide her astonishment at finding the Chieftain without the hood disguising his face.

Hale laughed. 'It's okay, you don't have to bow to me any longer.'

'He's my dad,' Simon said, and grabbed his father's arm.

Danice backed away in confusion. Her eyes flicked uncertainly from Simon to Hale. 'But, Simon, you told me your father was dead!' she said.

'That's because I thought he *was* dead,' Simon said. 'But he isn't. He's been here. And you've been working for him.'

'It's all been a disguise,' Hale explained. 'I'm in hiding from my own time. And I had to create an impression of power in order to live here.'

Danice stared at Hale for a long time, trying to make sense of what she'd been told. Then she took a deep breath. 'So, you're not from our time, and this has all been an act?' she said.

'Yes,' Hale replied.

'But you terrorised my whole family! Damien and I thought you'd kill us if we didn't do what you said!'

Hale looked grave. 'I'm truly sorry, Danice. I didn't want to cause you any suffering. But there was no other way. Please forgive me.'

Danice opened her mouth as if to yell at him. But she paused, and sighed. 'Well, now I'm not scared of you any more. And I'm glad my family won't have to go on any more missions.' She winced and turned to Simon. 'I'm sorry. I said all those rotten things about . . . the Chief . . . about your dad.'

Simon glanced at his father. 'It's okay. He deserved it.'

There was a renewed stutter of small-arms fire nearby.

Hale moved to Simon and took his shoulders with both hands. 'You're not going to like this, son, but I have to leave.'

'No, Dad!' Simon exclaimed. 'I just found you!'

Hale gazed down at Simon with all the warmth he could muster. 'The Tribunes won't show me any mercy, and you know better than anyone that the Time Bureau's hot on my trail.' He smiled. 'At least you know I'm not dead. I'm alive and kicking.'

'I won't tell them,' Simon said. 'I'll say I didn't find you. You could go to these Far Lands. Escape out there. But please don't go where I won't know where you are!'

'If you know where I am, it might get me out of the reach of the Tribunes. But it won't protect me from the Time Bureau. The Bureau is ruthless: it sent my own son to find me. It doesn't want time travellers it can't control.' He paused. 'And I'm not going to let them control me.'

'What about Mum and Lil?' Simon asked.

There was a welling of tears in Hale's eyes, which

he quickly blinked away. 'Don't worry, I'm sure they'll be all right.'

'You were going to tell me something about them . . . earlier. When we were down in the Seed Bank.'

'No time for that,' Hale replied. 'You'll find out soon enough.'

Simon felt panic rise in his throat. 'Then . . . tell me *where* you're going!'

'This may very well be my last journey, Simon. My body won't take much more. But I've found a safe place to hide—and to live.'

'Dad, no!'

'I can't tell you where I'm going. If you knew, don't you realise there are people out there who would stop at nothing to get what they want from you? I won't let them hurt you.' Hale drew Simon into a strong hug. He smiled at Danice. 'He's a good lad. Look after him, will you?'

Danice could only nod.

Simon took a moment to think. 'But, Dad, what about your Time Accelerator?' he said. 'What if someone else here gets hold of it?'

'That's all right, I've built in a self-destruct mechanism. It will activate a few minutes after I leave.' Hale looked at them both intently. 'Look, it would be best for you to make immediate plans to get away, too. How long's your mission time?'

'It was originally forty-eight hours,' Simon replied.

'We missed the scheduled pick-up but the TPS will return every eight hours.'

'Till they decide to cancel the operation,' Danice added.

'When's the next one due?' Hale asked.

Danice checked her wrist pilot. 'Dawn. Seven hours.'

'Then get back to the pick-up point. Lie low. Wait for extraction,' Hale said. 'Can you do that?'

'Sure,' Danice said. 'The only problem is getting there through all that trouble outside.'

'Dad, take me with you!' Simon pleaded one last time.

'No,' Hale said. 'I can't.' He lifted Simon's chin. 'Don't think badly of me for running off like this.' Then he handed Simon a folded note. 'And read this when I've gone.'

Simon took it, but he didn't trust himself to speak. He couldn't believe he was losing his dad for a second time. He clenched his teeth to make sure he didn't cry.

'Bye, son! Be careful.' Hale hesitated for a moment, then strode decisively to the next chamber and the elevator.

Simon followed for a few paces. 'Bye, Dad!'

Hale looked back through the doorway, nodded and stepped into the lift. A few seconds later the doors slid shut and he was gone.

Simon blinked back tears.

'It'll be all right,' Danice said. 'He must know what he's doing.'

'He's good at leaving,' Simon said bitterly. 'He knows how to do that, all right.'

'What does the note say?'

Simon unfolded the paper, not noticing a photograph fall out of it to his feet.

There was more gunfire outside.

'We don't have time for this now,' Simon said, and refolded the note. 'Our mission's over. Let's get back to the pick-up point so we can go home and report to the Bureau.'

Danice took the note away from him. 'Wait,' she said. 'This could be important.' She studied the note for a second before showing it to him. On it was a roughly drawn map with some scribbled writing in the margin.

'It's a diagram of the Seed Bank,' Simon said, looking closer, 'and this is Dad's writing. *Give to David*, it says. Who's David?'

'Maybe my father? His name is David,' Danice replied. 'But only my father's very close friends call him by his first name. Do you think my dad knows your dad?'

Simon shrugged. 'My dad seemed pretty pleased to hear that the Underground had captured an airship.'

'What! When?' Danice cried out. 'How did you know that?'

'It happened sometime today, during the riots in the city,' Simon said. 'Dad's offsider told us just a few moments ago.'

'That's been one of Bigdad's plans for a long time. To get an airship and go and explore the Far Lands.' Danice held up the map. 'Then this Seed Bank might have something to do with the Far Lands.'

'Dad told me the Seed Bank was meant as a gift to the people of your time. You think the gift is for y*our* dad?'

'It could be. If we get the chance, we'll ask him,' Danice replied.

'First, we'd better find a way to get out of here,' Simon said. 'It isn't going to be easy!'

Then he spotted something on the floor. It was a worn and wrinkled family photo of Hale, Glenda, Lil and himself. He grabbed it, stuffed it into his thigh pouch, and followed Danice outside.

32

A red glow lit up the night sky. An airship had crashed between the cave and the western wall of the fortress. It lay at a crazy angle, with tongues of flame and clouds of acrid smoke pouring from its crumpled fuselage.

'My dad's airship!' Simon said.

'I don't think so!' Danice pointed. 'They look like the Tribunes' men.'

The dark-uniformed bodies of four dead soldiers lay sprawled by the wreckage.

A few of Hale's guards still manned the rampart of the northern wall. But a dozen of Hale's men, in camouflage uniforms, had retreated from the wall to the cover of a cluster of rocks. They fired into the gap in the wall, where a gate had been smashed open by an armoured vehicle. It lay overturned beside the open gate, and the Tribunes' men were firing from the far side of the wall.

'How the heck are we supposed to get out of here?' Danice yelled.

A spray of bullets ripped across the compound and spattered the dust. A couple of the Tribunes' men appeared on the top of the western wall.

Simon glanced towards an empty section of the five-metre stone wall. There seemed to be no activity there, though that didn't mean anything. There could be soldiers on the far side. 'Look, if we want to get back to our pick-up point, we have to go west into the Big Forest. Let's try and get out over that way!'

'Springers over the wall?' Danice asked.

'No, too risky,' Simon said. 'We might drop into a pond!'

Danice ignored him. 'So, we climb it then?'

'We'll get closer and check it out,' Simon replied.

He started to run, keeping his head low. There was another explosion behind them.

Simon jumped over a dead guard and the blood-soaked ground around him. They reached the steps leading to the rampart on the western wall.

Danice suddenly shrieked a warning. 'Watch out!'

Three figures had clambered over the top of the wall and were jumping from the rampart directly above them.

Instinctively, Simon tackled the first and brought him struggling to the ground. Danice did the same with another.

Simon held his opponent down with all the weight of his body, while his right hand grabbed a rock from the ground. He lifted it, ready to smash it down again.

'Hey . . . hey . . . stop it!'

Simon hesitated. He dropped the rock. 'Nick! Is that you?' he gasped. He wiped the sweat from his eyes and looked down at the helmeted face.

'What do you think you're doing?' Nick yelled.

'What do you think *you're* doing?' Simon yelled back. 'I thought you were the enemy!'

'And you can get off me, too!' Taylor pushed Danice away with both arms and scrambled to her feet.

An intense surge of small-arms fire came from the northern wall.

'Get down, everyone!' Simon shouted. 'Get some cover!'

They dived into a depression in the ground, behind a stack of old timber and empty barrels. Ivan, Nick and Taylor activated their wrist pilots and retracted their helmets.

'What are you doing here?' Simon hissed.

'We're the cavalry,' Nick replied. 'We've come to rescue you!'

'Why did you appear outside the wall?' Danice asked.

'Our timeline actually appeared over there,' Nick replied, pointing to the northern wall. 'On the other side. That was your last reported position, near that gate.'

'Unfortunately, our wormhole appeared right beside a platoon that was firing mortars,' Taylor said, 'so we got away quickly and followed the wall round to here, to the western side.'

Simon peered out from behind a barrel to get a better view of the wall. 'Well, that still looks like the best way to escape.'

Ivan shook his head. 'Uh-uh, not now. A whole lot of soldiers followed us and they're massing outside. If they can't break through at that northern gate, I think they're planning to come over near here.'

There was sustained gunfire from the northern wall.

'And we're going to get killed if we sit around here talking!' Simon said. 'Follow me!'

A burst of bullets kicked up the dust as they ran across the open space and through the front entrance of the cave.

'Should we wait here?' Taylor said. 'Let things die down, and then try to get back over the wall.'

'I need some information first,' Simon said. 'The Bureau sent you guys to rescue us. But what were your exact instructions?'

'To locate you and Danice, return to the timeline, and evacuate,' Ivan replied.

Taylor checked her wrist pilot. 'The timeline's due to reappear in ten minutes for the pick-up.'

'I doubt the fight out there's going to be over that soon,' Simon said.

Danice gripped Simon's arm. 'Also, I can't leave from here. I have to know if Alli and Mama are all right. I have to get back to the forest first!'

Simon nodded. He understood the need for family more than ever. 'Okay. It looks like we can't use the timeline you three just arrived in,' he said to the others. 'It's not safe out there. And the Tribunes' men might overrun this place any minute.' He frowned in concentration as several plans fizzed in his brain. 'Answer me this . . . is the TPS that Danice and I used to get here still in emergency mode?'

'That's what we were told,' Ivan replied. 'It's on a set return pattern.'

Simon checked his wrist pilot. 'Then it's still due back on its eight-hour cycle at dawn. That gives us a lot more time to get out of here safely. I say that we get down to the forest so Danice can check her family's okay, and then we clear out on our own TPS. Everyone agree?'

They all nodded, except Danice, who shook her head.

'Do you have a better plan?' Simon snapped.

'It's just . . . maybe I won't go back. To your time, that is,' Danice said softly. 'I helped you here, showed you around. My job's over.'

Taylor stared at Danice in astonishment. 'But you're one of the team!'

'Hey, let's talk about this later,' Ivan said. 'Simon's plan sounds feasible. The question is, how do we get to the forest?'

'And still stay in one piece,' Nick added.

Simon had a sudden spark of inspiration. 'I think I've got an idea. Taylor's right. We should lie low for a while. So we'll go down in the elevator. It's over there!'

He pointed through the archway to the chamber beyond. 'I'll join you in a sec. I have to fetch something Dad left behind.'

He quickly left the main cave.

'Did I just hear him say "Dad"?' Taylor asked.

Danice paused. 'It's complicated . . .'

'How about the short version?' Taylor asked as they gathered outside the elevator.

'Well, Simon's dad left the Time Bureau in the twenty-first century. He escaped here. And became a kind of tribal chieftain . . .'

'Not this guy who's been plundering all the gold?' Nick asked.

'That's him,' Danice said. 'He started living here off and on last year, and he employed me and my brother and sister to pinch the gold so he could pay off the Tribunes. And now . . . he's gone again. And Simon has completed our mission. Now we go home. End of story.'

'So Simon's dad's the Chieftain!' Taylor said incredulously.

'That's cool,' Nick said. 'My dad's a Vision Control Officer.'

'A what?' Taylor asked.

'He cleans windows.'

'Ha, ha!'

'Hey, guys, focus,' Ivan said. 'Where's Simon? And where are we going next?'

'We're going down,' Simon said, coming back with his dad's Zone Relocator. 'And we should bring this with us.'

'What is it?'

'A new gadget,' Simon replied. 'Here's the elevator—let's go!'

A couple of minutes later, they emerged in the coolness at the bottom of the shaft.

'Is this where the Time Accelerator is?' Ivan asked.

'No,' Simon replied. 'We passed it on the way down. That's where Dad went.'

'Then what are we doing here?' Taylor asked.

Simon flicked a switch and the lights came on. 'Follow me—we're going to that room at the end of the tunnel.' Simon pointed to the steel door. 'We can hide out there until things settle down up top.'

They jogged down the tunnel to the door.

'Do you know the code?' Nick asked, tapping the electronic lock at the side of the door.

Simon hesitated. 'Um, I saw Dad punch it in. Four numbers.'

'His birthday? Sometimes people punch in the

numbers of the day and the month of their birthday,' Ivan suggested.

Simon nodded. 'Eleventh of October.'

'One—one—one—zero!' Nick said.

'Yeah, I can work it out—thanks!' Simon punched in the numbers. The door remained closed.

'Try all your family's birthdays,' Danice said.

As Simon punched in more numbers, a thunderous tremor shook the tunnel and the ground beneath.

'Get back! Into the doorway!' Simon yelled.

The temponauts squeezed their backs against the door. Another huge tremor shook the walls and ceiling, and jagged lumps of rock cascaded down. Choking clouds of dust filled the space and the temponauts covered their mouths.

'Activate helmets!' Ivan ordered.

A smaller shock trembled through the surrounding rock and the lights went off.

'What's happening?' Taylor cried out in the darkness.

'The Time Accelerator must have been blown!' Danice said.

'Activate helmet lights,' Ivan said.

The lights from their helmets projected into the dusty dimness.

'It was Dad!' Simon said despairingly. 'Those explosions . . . he's gone!'

'Simon, worry about it later,' Danice said. 'We have to get out of here. Let's get back to the elevator.'

Nick took the lead. The dust cloud filled the tunnel and made it almost impossible to see clearly.

'Watch out!' he warned. 'There are rocks everywhere!'

They picked their way slowly along the tunnel.

Nick suddenly stopped.

'Ouch! Hey! What's the hold-up?' the others said as they stumbled into him.

'Just stop!' Nick called out. 'I don't think we can go any further.'

There was a barrier of rocks between them and where the elevator should have been. Their lights focused on Nick as he scrambled up the sloping pile of rocks and touched the tunnel ceiling. He pulled a stone from the top of the pile, then another and another, and sent them rolling to the ground.

'It's blocked,' he said at last. 'Completely blocked to the ceiling. We'll never get through here!'

'We're trapped!' Danice groaned.

'There's nowhere to go!' Nick howled.

'Hey, you guys, look!' Simon called from a few metres back in the tunnel.

They turned, and their lights weaved around before fixing on Simon. He stood where a section of the tunnel wall had collapsed onto the floor. Simon clawed at the wall, scattering more rubble around his feet.

'What are you doing?' Ivan called out.

'Look! A door!' Simon called over his shoulder.

'What!' yelled the others.

They stumbled down the tunnel. Their lights shone on Simon, the wall and half of what appeared to be a black-painted sheet-metal door.

'Dad said these walls had been plastered with rocks and concrete lots of times over the years,' Simon said. He flicked open his Swiss Army knife and picked at the render. 'They must have covered over this door one of those times.'

Ivan poked a loose piece of wall and it dropped to the floor. 'Yeah, he's right. It's what they call blown render. Probably a bad mix of stones and concrete. And it's pretty old. It's no longer properly bonded to the rock underneath.'

The temponauts all stared at him.

'How could you possibly even know that?' Nick asked.

Ivan shrugged. 'My dad's in construction. You pick up a few facts here and there.'

'Thanks, Einstein,' Taylor said. 'Come on, this could be a way out. Let's dig.'

Their knives worked quickly on the crumbling render until they uncovered the entire door. Simon brushed away a layer of sandy concrete to reveal some red lettering.

'E . . . mer . . . gen . . .' Nick read as it became visible.

'Emergency,' said Simon as he brushed away the last of the dust.

'Exit!' they all yelled.

'But where does it go?' Ivan asked.

'Sounds like "out of here" to me,' Simon said. 'But let's try and open it first.'

'No code lock?' Danice asked.

'No. Pre-codes, I reckon. Must have a handle or something.' Simon looked to the right-hand frame of the door and halfway down. He picked away and uncovered a metal ring, fifteen centimetres in diameter and recessed in a circular metal casing.

'It's an iron pull-ring handle,' Ivan said. 'Just prise it out—and then we can give it a heave.'

Simon loosened the metal ring with his knife and swung it out.

'I'll hold onto the ring. You guys grab me and pull me back when I say,' Simon said. He gripped the metal ring with both hands. 'One—two—three!'

There was a loud creak but the door stayed fast.

'Again! One—two—three!'

The creaking was even louder. Suddenly, the door swung open and tore from its hinges.

'Let go of it!' Danice yelled.

They jumped back as it crashed to the floor.

'Rusty hinges, I reckon,' Ivan said.

Danice stepped forward to the doorway and peered in. '*Ugh!* Spiders!' She swiped away some trailing cobwebs and shone her helmet light into the space beyond. 'There's a tunnel here, too. Flat for a little way, then it starts to slope down. Quite steeply.'

'I still want to know where it goes,' Ivan said.

Danice turned around and tried to get her bearings. She looked down the tunnel to her right, where it was blocked. She turned a hundred and eighty degrees to the left. Then she turned again to the newly opened doorway.

'This is an emergency exit, right?' Danice asked.

'That's what it says.' Simon replied.

'How long's this place been here?'

'Back at the Time Bureau they said the nuclear power station was built over a hundred years ago. Dad said the Accelerator was built about the same time.'

Danice nodded. 'And maybe there weren't so many wild animals in the forest then.'

'So can you even make a guess where this tunnel goes?' Ivan asked.

Danice smiled. 'It goes to the Big Forest. If it's an emergency exit, it would be because people wanted to get out of here quickly and get some distance away. Judging by the direction it's going, I'd guess it leads right down to the base of the cliffs.'

Simon pushed past her and shone his light into the darkness. 'Then let's move.'

Twenty minutes later, Simon smelt fresh air. He shoved aside a pile of fallen branches that blocked the exit of the tunnel. 'Look,' he cried. 'We're out!'

Simon stepped into the open air amongst a jumble of boulders at the base of the cliff. He switched off his helmet lamp. Ahead of him towered the redwood forest. It was little more than a mass of black trunks and branches against the starlit sky.

The others emerged from the tunnel.

'*Whew!* Glad that's over!' Taylor said.

'It stank in there,' Nick added.

'Best thing is, we didn't need this,' Simon said. He took the Zone Relocator from the thigh pouch on his right leg.

'What *is* that?' Ivan asked.

'A Zone Relocator. One of my dad's most recent inventions,' Simon replied. 'It moves a timeline when you're out in the field, to wherever you want it.'

Taylor glared at him. 'You mean we could have used that in the tunnel—and got back home!'

'No,' Simon said. 'We promised Danice we'd get her back to her family.'

Danice gave him a grateful smile. 'I never even knew the tunnel was here,' she said. 'Our tree houses are just over that way.' She turned and pointed into the forest. 'But we have to go south-west to see Mama and Alli. They're at the Fire Caves!'

Nick looked nervously into the darkness. 'What, right now?'

'Look, everyone, the TPS appears at dawn at our former pick-up point,' Simon said. 'Maybe we should keep an eye on the time and head to the Fire Caves early in the morning.'

'You can relocate the TPS to there,' Ivan suggested.

'Exactly. For now, let's stay inside the tunnel entrance,' Simon said, glancing at Nick. 'We don't want to wander around in the forest at night, do we?'

'They told us about the wild beasts before we came here,' Nick said. 'I don't want to be tiger bait!'

As Simon sat down on the cold floor of the tunnel to rest, his thoughts kept returning to his father's departure. He wondered over and over again what he could have done to make his father stay. It was enough to send him crazy. He craved the oblivion of sleep, but it was a long time coming.

33

In the dawn light, Bigdad's stolen airship came into view, looming over the treetops.

'Grab those mooring ropes! Tie them to some tree trunks!' Damien said to a group of people who were waiting with him on the ground. He grabbed the end of a rope that dangled to within a metre of the ground where he, Alli and Hanna were waiting.

'Greetings!' Bigdad yelled as he slid out of the airship cabin.

Placing hand below hand, he climbed down the rope with a speed and dexterity that belied his bulky frame.

The arrival caused a flurry of activity through the forest. Dozens of people swarmed out of the Fire Caves with baggage hitched to their backs and small children in tow. They made their way to the clearing below the airship. On the ground, Bigdad stepped into the welcoming arms of his family.

'Have you seen Danice?' he asked.

'We've heard nothing,' Hanna replied.

Concern clouded Bigdad's eyes for a moment. But then he paused and looked at his family. 'Well, we captured it!' he said triumphantly, pointing up to the airship. 'Thanks to my men . . . and to Damien.' He grasped his son's shoulder warmly.

Damien grinned.

'It was touch-and-go there for a while, though,' Bigdad said. 'We got past the guard post, all right. Then we stumbled on a few soldiers up in the tower. They were watching the flames around the plaza, but we gave them some heat, too, didn't we, Damien? A quick tussle and we had them under control.'

'Shouldn't we get going, Bigdad?' Damien glanced warily in the direction of the faraway city. 'The fighting must be over by now, and the Tribunes will know the airship's gone. They might send soldiers out here, looking for us.'

Bigdad nodded and turned to the crowd who had gathered around. 'We haven't got much time,' he said. 'But we do have a ship! How many people are here?'

'About fifty,' Damien replied.

'We can take everyone, but we have to leave quickly.'

Suddenly Alli saw movement in the nearby trees. 'Look! It's soldiers! They've found us already!'

'It's too late!' a woman screamed.

Damien turned, reaching instinctively for the bow

and arrows strapped to his back. The shadows of two figures, then three, came darting through the trees.

Then one of them waved. 'Damien!' she cried.

Damien relaxed and he ran forward. 'Danice!'

'*Daa-neeece!*' Alli screeched. She ran across the clearing, leapt into her sister's embrace and wrapped her arms around her neck.

'*Agghh*, you're choking me!' Danice laughed.

'Danice! You're all right!' Bigdad strode across to her, lifted her easily and planted a kiss on her cheek.

'I'm fine! Put me down!' Danice protested. She pointed to the rest of the temponauts emerging from the forest. 'These are the guys I work with. Ivan, Taylor, Nick. And you already know Simon.'

'Welcome, welcome to you all,' Bigdad said.

Simon stepped forward. 'Thanks for helping us with those distractions in the city.' He glanced at the airship. 'I see you got your airship and that you got away okay.'

'I'm not sure we helped you much,' Bigdad replied. 'In fact, it was the trouble *you* caused out at the Prison Farms that really helped us. The Tribunes had to send more men from the city out there, leaving us almost free to do what we wanted.'

'You may not know, but the Tribunes sent a whole lot of troops to capture the Chieftain's fortress,' Simon said. 'They will have taken it by now.'

'And they won't stop there. They'll be after *all* their enemies after this,' Bigdad said.

'There's one other thing.' Simon handed him the map of the Seed Bank. 'I think this might be for you.'

Bigdad looked at it and raised his brows. 'A Seed Bank? You mean a repository of seeds?'

Simon decided to avoid any revelations about his father, and went for a simple explanation. 'The fighting got pretty fierce and the Chieftain decided to . . . get away . . . from the Tribunes, too. But he got together this huge collection of seeds. Wheat, barley, all sorts of useful plants. It's hidden inside a section of the cliff caves. The note says—*Give to David*.'

'We thought that might mean you,' Danice added.

'He must have known something about us. About our work in the Underground,' Bigdad said. 'Not surprising. My children worked for him, after all. Someone who could send people through time would have no trouble discovering a few local secrets, eh?' He folded the note and shoved it into his trouser pocket. 'We'll make use of this one day. Thank you.'

Taylor stepped forward. 'Sir, I have to convey an official communication to you,' she said formally. 'The Time Bureau is offering positions to Danice's brother and sister. If they want to continue their work as temponauts . . . with us in the twenty-first century.'

Alli grasped her father's hand tightly and shook her head. 'No, I'm staying here,' she said. 'I mean, I'm going with Bigdad and Mama.'

'There's your answer,' Bigdad replied. 'Damien?'

'Give me a minute,' Damien said. He took Danice by the elbow and drew her aside. 'What are you going to do?'

'It's hard,' she said, looking back at her family. 'I want to stay, but I'm getting an education in the twenty-first century, and doing things that I would never do here. You know, learning stuff that I never thought I'd know.' She glanced at the temponauts. 'And making some interesting friends.'

'You should stay with us! We're starting something new, too.'

'No, I can't,' Danice said. She took Damien's hands in both of hers. 'I know you're going to stay in this timezone. You're going to the Far Lands, aren't you?'

Damien smiled. 'First, tell me what happened to the Chieftain.'

'He's gone,' she said. 'To some other time. I don't know where.'

'Working with him was weird. I hated that guy,' Damien replied.

'I saw the Chieftain in a different light towards the end. It's not easy to explain . . . he wasn't who I thought he was,' Danice said. 'So, am I right about your plans?'

'You're right, Mama needs me.' Damien looked at his father. 'And I want to help settle our people in the Far Lands. Maybe even plan our return to the city one day, whatever happens.'

'Life's kind of interesting in other times, you know.'

'Well, don't forget I've seen a bit of that, too. Enough, maybe.'

'*Yoooo—eeeeee!*' A man gave an alarm call from the hatchway of the airship above.

Bigdad and the group looked up.

A young man lowered a brass telescope and shouted down, 'An airship! One of the Tribunes'. It's approaching us!'

'How far away?' Bigdad called back.

'Ten . . . fifteen minutes at the most!'

Bigdad sprang into action. 'We must go! Everyone aboard!' he shouted.

Ten ropes tumbled from the airship. People began climbing up with their bundled possessions.

'Wow, these dudes can climb!' Nick said, watching open-mouthed.

Danice rushed to her mother. 'Bye, Mama, bye!'

'Come with us!' Hanna pleaded.

Danice shook her head and hugged her, then turned to Bigdad. 'I have to go. It's what I want to do.'

Bigdad crushed her affectionately in his arms. 'Have a good life. Visit us if you can!'

Danice nodded, choking back tears.

Taylor turned to Simon. 'Unless we're planning to live here in the trees, how do *we* get out of here?'

Simon took the Zone Relocator from his travel pouch and checked his wrist pilot. 'Our emergency TPS will have appeared back at the original pick-up location three minutes ago!' He activated the

Zone Relocator. 'Give me the coordinates for here! Someone! Pronto!'

Ivan checked his wrist pilot and showed the screen to Simon. He punched in the coordinates and waited. The temponauts looked around hopefully. Nothing happened.

'Yeah, so what now?' Nick said.

'Hold on,' Simon said. 'Just wait.'

They made a strange and stationary group in the middle of the hectic sea of evacuation. Hanna, some of the older people and a few babies were being hauled up to the airship. Others crowded around the ropes, restlessly waiting their turn.

'Hurry, everyone!' the lookout cried from the airship. 'The other ship's getting closer!'

Ivan looked at the sky and back at Simon. 'Simon, is this gonna work?'

'Yeah!' Danice pointed. 'Look!'

The air started to spin between two trees. A bright pinpoint of light flared into a vortex. Then a sharp flash brought a TPS spinning into the space, and the wormhole reached its full clarity and size.

'Bigdad!' Danice yelled. 'We're going!'

From the airship above, the big man waved. At his side, Hanna looked down tearfully.

'The timeline won't stay open forever,' Ivan said.

Simon pushed Nick towards the wormhole. 'You first.'

Nick grinned. 'Neat gadget, surfie boy. See you at chow time!'

Suddenly he was gone.

Ivan tapped Taylor on the shoulder. She leapt into the void.

Danice was still staring intently at the airship. Damien stared back down at her.

'Bye, Damien!' she cried.

'See you!'

Alli waved from one of the cabin windows.

'Your turn, Danice,' Ivan said.

Danice lifted her arm and waved to the airship. Then she turned and dived into the wormhole.

'Now you,' Ivan said to Simon.

'It's my mission,' Simon replied. 'You go first!'

Ivan nodded and jumped.

Simon glanced in the direction of Old City. He took a deep breath. 'Bye, Dad,' he said, and stepped into the time tunnel.

34

'**H**ey, Simon, I've got a new mission for you,' Nick said, sliding a magazine across the table in the dining room at Mayfield Manor. 'Hawaii.'

Simon looked up from his baked beans. 'Why would I go there?'

'Hawaii!' Nick rolled his eyes. 'Surfing, of course! They reckon it started there hundreds of years ago. Take a look at those waves!'

'Looks good,' Simon said tonelessly. Normally he would have loved to chat with Nick about surfing, but right then, he couldn't seem to get excited.

Ivan stood up. 'Officer present!' he said.

'Relax, take it easy, you're on Down Time!' Captain Cutler said as he strode into the room.

'Thanks, sir,' Danice replied. She picked up a jug of orange juice and a glass. 'Want a drink, sir?'

Cutler pulled out a chair and sat down. 'No, thank you. But I wouldn't mind an answer.'

'Taylor's the smart one,' Nick replied. 'She knows everything, sir.'

'Yeah, I know you need a better deodorant,' Taylor muttered.

Nick sniffed his armpit and pretended to collapse headfirst into his empty soup bowl.

'Ladies, gentlemen, please,' Cutler continued, tossing a report onto the table. 'I've had a memo from the History Unit. It seems that the word *saucepan* is starting to appear, in England, in the early to mid-seventeenth century. Years before it was supposed to. We've had several missions to that time. Can anyone give me an explanation?'

Cutler looked from one face to the next, awaiting a response. 'Spenser?'

'No, sir. Not me, sir!'

'Anyone else?' His eyes fixed on Simon, who was pushing a bean around the plate with his fork. 'Savage?'

Simon thought about his answer and of his father's words—'*We are always changing things when we time travel*'. The thoughts of his father reminded him of everything that had happened in the twenty-fourth century, and suddenly, the Bureau's concern about the historical name for a cooking pot seemed petty and irrelevant.

'No, sir, no idea at all,' he answered.

Danice stared at him and poured herself another glass of juice.

'A bit of a mystery, then,' Cutler said.

'Time's a mystery to us all,' Nick said helpfully.

'Thank you, Spenser, very illuminating,' Cutler said, getting up from his chair. 'Enjoy your evening. By the way, a stack of new movies have come into the library.'

Nick and Danice immediately rose from their seats. Simon stayed where he was.

'Savage, a word with you?' Cutler added. 'In my office, please.'

Simon looked at the others, raised his eyebrows, and followed the captain.

'They've got a new job for you!' Nick called out. 'Eel-keeper!'

Simon left the room with their laughter ringing behind him. He barely heard it.

'Take a seat,' Captain Cutler said as they entered his office.

'I've had my debriefing, sir, two days ago,' Simon said. 'When I got back from the mission.'

'This isn't a debrief,' Cutler replied. 'Sit down.'

Simon wondered if he was in trouble. 'Can I ask something first?' he said.

'Go ahead,' Cutler replied, leaning back in his swivel chair.

'You knew my father was there, didn't you?' Simon said. 'In the twenty-fourth century.'

'We suspected it, yes,' Cutler said. 'The chances it was anyone else were very slim.'

'And you knew how he left the beach at Kiama on that day?'

Cutler nodded. 'Yes.'

Simon hesitated. 'I have to know. Are you the one who tipped him off, sir? Rang him in Sydney, early in the morning, Australian time? From here?'

Cutler's expression gave nothing away. 'That's not for me to say. But it would have been a disaster if those military personnel had got hold of him.'

'That means yes.'

'That means whatever you want to believe, Simon,' Cutler replied.

'Okay, sir. Thank you. Can I ask you one more thing?' When Cutler nodded, Simon went on. 'What was my real mission?'

Cutler smiled. 'To establish the source of power and the location of the Time Accelerator. To discover the true identity of the Chieftain. You did all that we asked. And that Zone Relocator you brought back was a major bonus.' He paused. 'Of course, it also gave you the opportunity to find your father.'

'Sir . . . what's the Bureau going to do about him?'

Cutler considered his reply. 'There's a lot at stake here, Simon. Powerful time technology that the world has never seen before. And power that should stay in the control of a single organisation.'

'You mean the Time Bureau, sir?'

'Yes. I do.'

'And Dad?'

'We'll do whatever we have to, to keep this power in *our* hands.'

'So you'll keep looking for him,' Simon said. 'You'll . . . you'll . . .'

'We'll do whatever we have to,' Cutler said. 'That's all I can say.'

They're going to search for Dad across time, Simon thought. And they won't stop till they find him. And then what? *Would they kill him?*

'Now can I ask you something?' Cutler said.

Simon focused back on the captain. 'Sure, sir.'

'Have you heard from your mother and sister lately?'

'No. Not since before my mission.'

'What I have to tell you concerns them.'

'What is it—*an accident*?'

'No,' Cutler said, 'but you reported in the debriefing that your father has disappeared to another time and set himself up there. And that, allegedly, he wouldn't tell you where.'

Simon began to feel uncomfortable. What was Cutler getting at? 'Yeah, that's right, sir,' he said.

Cutler took a disk in a paper sleeve from his desk. 'We received a message today. From your father.'

Simon blinked. 'How?'

'It came right up in front of us on the Operations Screen. Another one of his smart tricks!'

'Wh-what does it say?'

'Well, there were two messages really. There was one for us. And this one is for you.' Cutler tapped the disk. 'Your father informed us that, after he disappeared from the twenty-fourth century, he made one trip to the twenty-first century. To our time. In the last forty-eight hours.'

'Here? Why?'

'To see your mother and sister. But what I have to tell you, Simon,' said Cutler, leaning against the desk, 'is that your mother and sister have disappeared.'

'What do you mean, sir? Where?'

Cutler shrugged. 'I only wish we knew. Your father simply tells us that they're with him. Wherever he's gone.'

'He's, like . . . taken them!'

'Yes. You could say that. Although they went willingly, we presume.'

'Didn't we pick up the timeline, sir, before or during his arrival?' Simon asked.

'No. It seems that your father's developed a cloaking device for timelines. We can't find the one to the house in Bristol where your mother and sister lived. We can't uncover the one to wherever he's gone now. Not yet.'

The news sunk in slowly.

I have to think like they think in the Bureau, Simon told himself. Think strategically. Don't panic. Don't fly off the handle.

How could he best help his father, his mother and Lil? They were more important to him than anyone in the Time Bureau. It was because of them that he'd come to the Bureau in the first place.

It was a full minute before Simon spoke again. 'Sir, what are my options?' he asked.

'Spoken like a true Bureau man,' Cutler replied. 'Well, you can return to Bristol, and live with your grandparents. It's not Australia, I know, but it would be something like a normal life.'

Suddenly the unfairness of the whole situation hit Simon. This was more than anyone should have to cope with at thirteen. He should be worrying about schoolwork, surfing and girls, not about a fugitive father who was battling to stay free of people who wanted to control his ideas. Or about the Time Bureau people who pretended to care about Simon, but who really wanted to use him against his own father. But if he walked away from it all, he might never see his family again. He decided to hear what Cutler had to say.

'Yes, sir. I could go to Bristol. Or . . .?'

'Or . . . you can help us find your mother and sister. And help us find your father. Stay in the Bureau. Become one of *us*.'

Simon thought it over. He already knew too much. How safe would he be back in civilian life? Would the Bureau simply let him walk away? Or would he be found dead one day? From some sort of accident?

It didn't matter. His priority was Lil and Mum . . . and Dad. He had to stay in the Bureau in order to find them.

'Sir, I want to stay,' Simon said.

'I was hoping you'd say that,' Cutler replied, 'but the search could be long and difficult. Can we count on you?'

'One hundred per cent,' Simon said.

'Then I'm authorised to give you this.' Cutler handed him the disk. 'It's the message from your father.'

'Thank you, sir.'

'Normal duties resume tomorrow morning. Six a.m. Sharp!'

'Sir! Yes, sir!'

35

In Simon's room, Hale's face appeared on the screen of his laptop. Simon zipped up the volume and clicked *PLAY*.

His father smiled.

'Simon, I hope the reception is okay. I know that if you are watching this, then the Time Bureau has seen it, too. However, I had to get a message to you.' He paused. 'I didn't mean to surprise you like this. By now you'll know about Mum and Lil. Sorry, I couldn't tell you. I couldn't let anyone know of my intentions. All I can tell you is this: we're in another place and we're safe and we're well.' His gaze flickered away momentarily to something beyond the camera, and then back again.

'Well, we're okay for now. As I told you, I have uncovered some of the great secrets of time and how it works. But I have to protect these secrets. Simon . . . find me if you can. There are clues if you look closely enough. And if you choose to follow them.' Then he smiled again. 'Find me, and maybe some of my secrets will be yours, one day. Farewell, son. I'm proud of you. Live well!'

The image faded.

Simon slumped onto his bed. He was still dog-tired from the mission and he needed another long night of deep sleep. He had never felt so hollow or lost. But he knew he had to get over it or he might as well give up now.

He glanced up to the wrinkled photo on the noticeboard . . . the smiling faces of a once-happy family. Simon picked up his clock, set the alarm for five-thirty and listened to its rhythmic tick.

'I'll find you,' he said to the photo. 'I'll get there first. I promise.'

36

At a late-night conference, Professor McPhee and Captain Cutler stared carefully at the Timeline Operations Screen in the Command Centre.

'This next mission's a dicey one,' McPhee said. 'And I want someone to go tomorrow.'

'Where's it to?' Cutler asked.

'France, fifteenth century. It involves a lot of soldiers, a lot of experts with the crossbow.'

'Then we need someone who can get in and out quickly,' Cutler said. 'And who isn't afraid to think on their feet.'

'We need our best operative,' McPhee said.

'No question, then,' Cutler said.

McPhee nodded. 'We'll send Simon Savage.'

Acknowledgements

In writing this book, I would like to thank the following people for their kind assistance and advice: Kory Hearn, Helen Nolan, Allicia Stadon, Bethany Watt, Fiona Carruthers, Belle and Larry Buttrose, Nerine Martini, Caroline Stanton, Rachel Skinner, Cheryl Tornquist, John Stephenson, Alex Paige and other esteemed members of the Carringtonians. I'd also like to thank Sigrid Jagusch and the food and coffee brigade at the Red Door Cafe, Leura. As always, the neighbourhood cat, Martin, has taken a keen interest in the progress of this book, and in my kitchen leftovers.

Thanks also to Rod Hare, Margrete Lamond, Kate Mayes and Libby Volke at Little Hare Books and to my agent, Rick Raftos. The author is grateful to Professor Geoffrey Blainey for his *Very Short History of the World* which proved a most useful resource on the epochs of humanity. The author now promises to become even more informed by reading the longer 'short' version.

Coming soon . . .

SEND
SIMON
SAVAGE
Return of the Black Death

Simon Savage, the temponauts and the Time Bureau are on full alert. The Black Death has started to appear in major cities around the world. There are fears of a global pandemic.

The plague has been carried to the present time by the fleas on rats from the fourteenth century. But who is behind this deadly scheme?

The Time Bureau has its suspicions. Simon, Danice, Ivan, Nick and Taylor face a long struggle across the eons with a sinister group of time travellers known as the Shadowers.

Meanwhile, Simon must find his family. Where have they gone? Will he be able to unravel the clues to their disappearance? Can he protect them from the Time Bureau itself?

The adrenalin-pumping action continues in *Send Simon Savage—Return of the Black Death.*

About the Author

Stephen Measday has spent his life writing books, scripts, plays and poems, and occasional advertising slogans for his father's pharmacy.

Stephen's ancestors voluntarily left Sandwich in England in 1854 and settled in South Australia where they helped out the barefooted by making shoes and boots.

Over a century later, Stephen grew up in a faraway country town and went to work in Adelaide as a reporter, before deciding to take up full-time writing as a profession.

He now lives in the Blue Mountains, outside Sydney, where he collects books, goes bushwalking, watches cricket, reads about rare animals and dreams of safaris in Africa.

Stephen hopes that *Measday* will one day be recognised as the official eighth day of the week.

Send Simon Savage is his sixteenth book and he intends to write some more. *So watch out!*

Praise for
Send Simon Savage

'The whole book was a great read! To sum this book up in one word is easy: Brilliant.'   *—Tiana Bryce*

'This book is totally random and mystifying. I hope there will be a second.'   *—Jacob Harris*

'My son loved the book. I am going to have to read it, too!'   *—a reader's mum*

'A fast-paced read with all the gadgets (love the bio-dynamic suits), close calls and adventure any thrill seeker could want.'   *—Steve Howard*

'. . . this fast-paced action thriller is hard to put down.'   *—Bookseller+Publisher Magazine*

'Very similar to Matthew Reilly's books, *Send Simon Savage* offers . . . plenty to share and enjoy.'   *—Bookseller+Publisher Magazine*